Book 1, Pale Moonlight

By Marie Johnston

Porter Denlan's home is in turmoil, his pack lives in fear of their cruel leader, but he knows one female whose birthright can govern them without question. Unfortunately, his nemesis is also searching for her—and it isn't to bring her back to the home she was taken from.

Raised as a human, Maggie Miller wishes she could connect with her species. But when a sexy carpenter makes outrageous claims about her destiny, she blows him off—despite her intense attraction toward the rugged male. Hours after she watched his admirable backside walk out, three brutes attack her. Unable to stay away from her, Porter jumps to her aid; they barely escape.

On the run, they learn what Maggie's birthright truly is—and how it could tear them apart.

For every book, there are so many people to thank and I truly appreciate each and every one. Writing began as a solo endeavor and with each book, I realize how important having a team is. The first member of my team, my husband, has been one of the most critical. Without him running interference between the kidlets and the daily grind, my writing time would be next to nil. His support and enthusiasm have kept me going through the ups and downs of this business.

We make a good team, my dear.

Chapter One

The only reason Porter Denlan wasn't a tuft of fur in the breeze was because his death would be too obvious, too convenient. But soon, it wouldn't matter.

Sitting in Town Hall, he fumed while listening to a power hungry psycho speak at the podium. The speaker's best interest wasn't for the town, Lobo Springs; his primary concern wasn't for the people of the quaint, woodsy village. And that was a shame because he was their leader.

Porter never whispered about his opposing thoughts of Seamus Meester's leadership choices. Instead, he was vocal and well witnessed—always. As one of the six clan heads under Seamus' rule, he ensured none of his pack spoke against the male. As the resident carpenter, Seamus had never viewed him as more than a burr in his paw.

What Seamus didn't know would soon hurt him.

Switching his focus to the asshole at the podium only made Porter want to tear the wooden stand down, plank by plank. To think, he'd built the thing Seamus snidely spoke behind.

"Denlan is correct. Our new government, the TriSpecies Synod, granted each shifter colony the option to vote in their leadership. However, it does not mean we *need* to change our ways. We have six clans, each with a capable leader…" he threw Porter a side-eye, suggesting maybe one of the clans' heads wasn't, "we have functioned as such for a quarter of a century. Did I not bring Lobo Springs into current times with the name change and all of our advancements?"

Porter snorted in derision. Seamus narrowed his focus on him. The former name, Great Moon, had been a name worthy of a shifter colony, and in no way dated or suggested that it was any different than a human town.

Seamus increased the volume of his rough voice until it boomed off the walls. "This town was on the brink of bankruptcy when I took charge. Now you see new stores opening, a library full of books, and our cars no longer sit on the side of the road in disrepair."

While he could claim that success and be accurate—he was a money savvy bastard—it didn't mean the townsfolk had free access to new technologies like wireless internet. Not unless they had a special connection to Seamus or carried out certain favors.

"Proof alone," Seamus' tone dropped low, "that *I* am a worthy leader of the colony."

The figurative dead horse lay in front of Porter, but he beat away on it. "If we have the chance to vote," he said, biting each word out, "we'll find out how the shifters of each clan feel about the way the colony is run."

"So far," Seamus' lips turned up smugly, "the only shifter I see complaining…is you. How far would you have us carry this voting business, Denlan? Do we elect clan leaders next?"

Ah, the slick prick knew how to play the crowd, from the way he spoke to his styled russet hair and silk ties adorning his business suits. Other clan leaders might fear losing their standing if their members were allowed to vote. Porter didn't fear his position like the others did. Those of the packs that made up his clan trusted him implicitly, like they had his father.

"We have an opportunity to advance, to move forward with the world around us. It's necessary to blend in with humans." Porter paused to look each one of the representatives in the eye. "It's necessary to keep up with the vampires."

Grumblings wafted through the stale air in the room. Porter knew his remark hit them where it counted. Vampires and shifters may have united in government and species' security, but the old colonies, the rule-with-an-iron-fist-and-hide-behind-tradition ones like Lobo Springs, resisted as aggressively as possible. They may have accepted satellite TV and Netflix, but it didn't mean behaving like humans and doing absurd events like elections.

"We do not follow the herd like fangers." Typical Seamus move, using shifter pride against them. Typical shifters, it would work. "The Synod leads us, provides council, we follow their laws. No reason to change."

Porter wanted to howl, but he wasn't given to chasing his baser instincts. His wolf demanded release, to challenge Seamus like the old ways, but Porter preferred higher thinking. It's what made their previous ruler a better leader than Seamus "Kill Them if They Don't Agree With Me" Meester.

"You are dismissed, Denlan." Seamus' hard voice resonated, quieting any mumblings from the clan representatives.

Porter sneered at all of them, lingering the longest on Seamus. All eyes dropped away in a sign of deference—and shame.

The glint of hard steel in Seamus' green eyes promised retribution. If Porter was a cat, he'd be on life seven-point-five. *That's right. Think about killing me, and how you can't because for once it'd be obvious it was you.*

Unlike their leader, Porter used his carpentry skills for the people, often not charging for repairs. He didn't conduct business like Seamus by holding it over their heads until they loaned him their daughter for the night. His vocal objections often tamed Seamus' violent tendencies because one, Porter's work kept him in peak physical shape and Seamus was slightly threatened. Two, Porter was so well-liked within the village that Seamus couldn't retaliate by killing him without inciting questions that he'd gone feral.

It made Porter consider offing himself and framing Seamus. If only Porter could risk leaving his pack at the mercy of Seamus orchestrating who he wanted to take Porter's place if he challenged the male and lost.

***

Maggie Miller waved goodbye to her coworkers as they all scattered like marbles rolling downhill. Her favorite part about Fridays was that she had two whole days of *not* working at the daycare center. As an adult, she still hadn't answered the question of what she wanted to be when she grew up, but it certainly wasn't a preschool teacher.

She loved the kids. They were the only reason she survived each day. Their energy helped her run her own levels down. The fidgety preschoolers had nothing on her; she was always so *restless*.

Blame it on biology.

During the routine drive home, she calculated the time she'd need to get to her other job. Freemont was coming alive with the weekend crowd. She watched them with keen shifter eyes, evaluating who was out for fun, who was out for mischief, who was out for no good. A habit of hers she'd developed as a teenager. Instincts she'd been acting on for a few years.

As she drove into the underground parking garage of her apartment complex, her phone rang.

One guess who was calling her on a Friday night.

"Hey, Ma," she answered, maneuvering into her assigned parking spot.

"Maggie," her mother's raspy voice greeted in return. "I made too much for dinner if you'd like to come over."

Same thing, different Friday night. Her mother worried that she lived on her own. Fretted that she might go out after dark.

They were *shifters*, for fuck's sake! Darkness was when they came alive and roamed the city looking for company to get carnal with.

The others out after sunset should be scared of *her*.

"Sorry, Ma. I just picked up something to eat and ordered a movie on pay-per-view I've been dying to see. I was really looking forward to a quiet night in. Work was especially chaotic today. It's always that way the week of daylight savings time."

"Oh." Her mom's disappointment was palpable—and meant to inspire enough guilt to change her mind.

Maggie clued into her manipulations years ago. Armana Miller had contrived so much of Maggie's life, took her away from their people to live in the human world, and drove away her brother, Jace. He was the only male who had ever been a part of her life and he was as good as dead to her. As her only family left, Maggie appeased her mom and practiced escape and evade tactics to safeguard as much freedom as possible. Like lying over the phone so she couldn't scent Maggie's deception.

"Do you want to come over tomorrow?" Hope dripped from each word.

Deep mental sigh. "Sure. An early dinner?" Because she had plans for tomorrow night, too. Ones her mother didn't need to know about.

"Absolutely. I bought an excellent roast. I can sear it and we'll dig in."

The rarest of rare. Maggie's empty stomach rumbled its approval. Her mother might irritate the shit out of her, but the female could cook. Roasts, bacon wrapped meatloaf, rib night…

Every time she cut into one of her mother's rare cuts of meat, she marveled that the shifter female hadn't adapted to the well-doneness humans preferred, too.

It was comforting to know there was at least one limit to her mother's human assimilation.

"I'll be there at four. Love ya, Ma." Maggie waited for the automatic "love you, too" response and disconnected before her mother mothered even more.

She took the stairs two at time to her third floor flat and burst through her door. She had thirty minutes to change and get to her second job.

Shedding her chevron-print maxi skirt and billowy shirt, she tossed them into the laundry. Next went her bra and underwear. All the items were comfortable and hid her sensual figure—and that's why they were absolutely wrong for where she was headed.

She shook her long, mahogany hair out of its twist, running her fingers through it. Out of her closet she grabbed a red leather corset, tight red pants that hugged every inch of her rounded hips and muscular thighs. Black stilettos that tied up her ankles completed the ensemble, but she'd lace those before she left.

The dickwads living below her called management and complained whenever she walked around wearing them.

Sometimes she wished she'd brought her dates home. Let management bluster their way through an explanation of that bitch session.

Brushing her hair into a sleek, dark shine to lay over one shoulder, she decided on her makeup. The smoky eye went really well with her pale blue eyes. Three layers of mascara and blood red lipstick and she was barely recognizable as the preschool teacher who ran around the playground.

With two faux diamond studs and a pair of serpent wraparound earrings, she braced herself. Individually, she shoved each one through the tender skin of her ear lobe. Wincing slightly, she was accustomed to the pain. Her shifter blood healed her body so fast, just changing styles required a new piercing. They didn't fit her daycare persona, so she chose to puncture a pair in whenever necessary.

She'd love a tattoo, maybe one along her hipbone to peak out the top of her skirt, but the cost of silver-laced tattoo ink was well out of her price range. Anything less and her shifter skin would heal and wipe out the ink. To compensate and add flair to her appearance, she lined each wrist with sparkly bangles

Twenty minutes before her shift started and it took fifteen to get to the edge of town for work. She grabbed a long grey coat out of her closet, threw it on, snatched her shoes and sprinted back down the stairs.

Pulling up to work with minutes to spare, she crammed her feet into the fuck-me heels, yanked the ties up, and trotted inside as quickly as possible in sky-high shoes.

The girl at the counter of The Gift Shop glanced up, then at the clock. "Cuttin' it close, Miller."

"Is she still here?" Maggie shrugged off her coat. The shop was empty, but they hadn't entered prime shopping time for the specialty store.

"In the back. Here." Vanessa's French-tipped manicure clacked away on the computer as she logged out and turned the screen to Maggie. "Hurry and log in. You've got a minute before you're officially late."

Maggie's boss put any bitch to shame—shifter or human. Brenda Higgins ruled the novelty sex shop with a twenty-four carat gold fist. She knew the industry inside and out, had been in the sex business in some form her entire adult life. Mrs. Higgins wasn't afraid to change with the times. The Gift Shop's online business more than supplemented the steady flow of the shop.

"Done." Maggie hit enter on her login, grinning at Vanessa. The human could be considered a friend. Not that she could get close to any.

The whole I-could-turn-into-a-wolf detail created distance in any friendship with humans.

"It's gonna be a busy night. I'll be home all night. The hubs is home, too, so call if you need help." Vanessa rolled her eyes to the back room. "I doubt you'll get any otherwise."

"Is she staying all night?" Maggie whispered.

Vanessa shrugged. "Doubt it, but you know how she likes to hover. Anyway, I have to pick Tanner up from daycare. Later."

The girl loved working at the shop. Vanessa and her husband tested each toy, and she had become the go-to expert on all things erotic. Her first-hand knowledge and people skills earned her a nice wage from Mrs. Higgins.

Maggie…not so much.

She had only mild interest in sex toys, lubes, or restraints. The majority of her knowledge came from listening to Vanessa dispense advice. It wasn't that she scorned them, but shifters weren't known for their patience and many of the items she sold required more than a hormonal urge and a willing body. Very few shifters frequented the store.

Maggie anticipated that would change. She predicted that once her kind experienced the pleasure sexual devices could bring and the dominance certain items promised, the store's profit would double.

"Maggie." Mrs. Higgins strode in. How she managed to look down her nose at Maggie who stood a good six inches taller than her—before she put her heels on—was a skill the woman had mastered completely.

"Hey, Mrs. Higgins." Thank goodness her human boss couldn't smell emotions because insincerity dripped off Maggie.

Mrs. Higgins eyes narrowed. Still, the woman possessed some weird sixth sense. She'd only hired Maggie because she was desperate. Maggie tolerated their less desirable clientele and didn't scare off easily. She also didn't complain about working nighttime weekend hours.

Mrs. Higgins constantly ensured Maggie knew she'd been a last resort.

As if Maggie cared. She didn't need this job for monetary reasons. Preschool teachers didn't rake in a sweet wage, but it paid rent, her car payment, and bought groceries.

Her job at The Gift Shop was necessary for other reasons. It soothed her antsy soul.

For the next twenty minutes, Maggie was put through "the quiz" where Mrs. Higgins grilled her about the novelties the store offered.

Maggie threw Mrs. Higgins a curve ball. "The strawberries and cream edible panties taste like sugared plastic." She grinned at the shock registering on her employer's face.

Much of Mrs. Higgins distain was Maggie's perceived innocence. If only the boss lady knew. Maggie couldn't rattle off how well anal plugs stayed in place, or the true effectiveness of Benwa beads, but she couldn't claim purity.

She was a shifter with all their urges—as much as her mother pushed her otherwise. Isolated from her species, she knew next to nothing about her kind, but she learned all about how different she was from the people surrounding her every day of her life.

"Have you sampled the flavored lubes?" The woman's eyes almost crossed with her superior expression.

"I bought the sampler pack. The chocolate one's nothing like a Lindor truffle, but I guess it's better than cock flavor."

The corner of Mrs. Higgins mouth quirked. "Indeed."

Score. Maggie could win over the old maid yet.

With a regal nod and a few more instructions, Maggie was finally alone.

Customers filtered into the store. Ladies asked her questions, guys asked her opinion, and two dudes gave her their phone numbers.

Those she held onto. When the urge came on, it was good to have contacts. Human males lacked the stamina she required, but they scratched an itch. Whatever need remained after their interlude, well…she had access to plenty of self-pleasuring devices. With an added bonus that she'd have more answers for Mrs. Higgins.

A bachelorette party came in, giggling and snickering over the items they bought for the future bride. Those types had irritated Maggie at first, but she'd grown to truly enjoy them. Youthful, excited for the future, supporting each other…all things that had been taken away from her.

While helping them, the door dinged with another customer. Maggie didn't have to look up to know.

He was here. The guy Maggie waited for.

He wore slacks, a button-up striped shirt, and a crooked tie. His hair hung limp on his forehead. She had no idea what he did for a living, but she knew him for what he was as soon as he'd entered the shop a few weeks ago.

In the back room, he picked through the videos available for rent. Like the other times he'd been in, he perused the selection but came out empty-handed.

Scanning the traditional vibrators and cock rings, he made his way to the edible undergarments. He always bought those.

His behavior wouldn't be unusual—to a human. Normal dudes didn't smell like him: seedy, dirty, wrong. It was the smell of a sexual predator. A scent Maggie had imprinted on her brain over a decade ago.

What the man didn't know was that he wasn't the only predator in the room.

She finished with a customer, acutely aware of the man. Last time he'd paid with cash and she'd missed the flash of his address on his license when he'd opened his wallet. He wouldn't use a credit card. Too easy to track the purchase if his victim ever sought help, or if he ever went too far and the victim *couldn't* seek aid.

"How's your Friday going?" She used a cheery tone as he approached to pay.

His gaze rose from her cleavage. "Good."

He wasn't a talker. Some of them were. Targeting her while chatting, evaluating if she was an easy catch. The Gift Shop was her best chance for hunting men like Edible Panties Guy. Sure, predators were everywhere, but at the store, they came to her often enough to keep her busy.

"That'll be twenty-nine, ninety-two." *Please hold your wallet open.*

The wallet opened, the slot holding his license faced away from her.

Dammit.

He pulled out a twenty and ten. Before he closed the wallet, she made her move.

Grabbing the store's business card, she tucked it into the middle slot, exerting enough force to tip the wallet back. "Here's our online store information. There's a wider variety available than what we carry in the store." She leaned over, arching her back, her breasts nearly falling out to grab his attention. Her heightened eyesight picked out his address.

She straightened, flashing a radiant smile. "Enjoy your night."

Her bust stung from his leer.

The rest of the night went so damn slow. Five minutes before close, a customer entered and took her sweet ass time—naturally. Finally, Maggie was done with work, the store was closed. Time to begin the hunt for Wally Donaldson, four-twenty-one Sycamore Lane.

Chapter Two

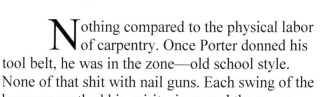

Nothing compared to the physical labor of carpentry. Once Porter donned his tool belt, he was in the zone—old school style. None of that shit with nail guns. Each swing of the hammer soothed his spirit, simmered the anger threatening to take over, allowed him time to think. And plan.

He continued work on the library's basement renovations because he needed to hit something, motivated by memories of the vampire attack on their colony twenty-five years ago. The entire village remembered; no one spoke of it. Their beloved leader, Bane Troye, had been slain, along with his oldest son, Keve. In the aftermath, the widow had fled with her two younger kids, leaving Seamus the opening he'd sought for so long.

If Porter could go back and throttle the widow he would. Seamus had caused problems for years, since Porter was old enough to understand pack politics. Then *she* left with the last Troye blood relatives. A brutal fight of prospective leaders had left only Seamus standing.

Porter's father was one of the slain.

Slamming a two-by-six down, Porter yanked out his measuring tape. Framing a wall rested high on his pleasurable list. Any prospective female in the village paled against the satisfaction of a newly built wall measuring square after the first try.

Means you haven't found the right female, Porter, he heard his father's rumble. One of the many pieces of sage advice he'd dispensed Porter over their projects, special father-son bonding.

Sweet Mother Earth, he missed that guy. His mother had been killed in the vampire attack. Porter had been grief-stricken, but it was a drop in an ocean compared to her mate. His father had been emotionally flayed open, dying slowly with each passing minute, his soul yearning to seek peace with his eternal mate.

If his father had won the challenge with Seamus, he might have found the will to go on, the responsibility of the village enough to keep him going. Instead, he'd held back, not fighting to his full potential, a form of suicide, really, and Porter witnessed how easily a shifter as brutal as Seamus could rip a heart out.

Porter kicked another board into position, squatting down to nail it in place.

How long had he been wracking his mind for a way to remove Seamus Meester from Lobo Springs future?

An image of an aggressive, mulish, bad-tempered cocksucker popped into his head. Jace Stockwell.

It had taken Porter forever to track down the oldest surviving child of Bane Troye. Until a few years ago when he'd heard about a Jace Stockwell who'd been made a Guardian, the law enforcement of their people.

Porter had tracked Jace to the shifter nightclub, Pale Moonlight, where he'd worked before becoming a Guardian. He'd talked with Jace, his goal to persuade him to come home and claim his Great Moon lineage and boot Seamus out. Not even Seamus could argue with birthright, especially from as beloved a leader as Troye had been.

Troye is my history. My mate and the Guardians are my future. Don't ever come around asking me about it, or my family, again.

Porter's legendary level head had taken a vacation after he heard those words. The club's owner hauled him out before he incited a riot from the emotions roiling off him.

A growl escaped. His hammer slipped, the nail pinging away to skitter across the floor. A forty-degree bend in the rod-shaped metal ruled it out for being used again.

Swearing under his breath, Porter reached for another nail only to find his pouch empty.

Hell, it was lunchtime anyway.

"Duuude, you fighting with yourself down here?" His best friend and fellow pack member, Sanders Claude stomped down the stairs.

"Yeah, I kinda am. This remodel is going longer than planned." *Because I'm going slow as hell.*

"I understand. Heard there were some intense discussions during the Town Hall meeting." Sanders leaned against the railing.

Porter wouldn't recommend it. His friend might find himself on his ass when the rickety screws gave out. The lower level of the library he renovated needed the update badly. It had been the easiest gutting he'd ever done; everything was already falling apart. "It was *one* discussion, and it was shut down too quick to be intense."

He hooked his hammer into his tool belt and unstrapped the entire contraption. Setting it by his tool box, he circled around to pick up the rest of his tools.

"I stopped by to see if you needed some help. Or needed to talk where keen ears couldn't hear."

Pushing his hair off his face, Porter realized that, yes, he had some things to run across Sanders. No one knew about his investigation into the Troye survivors, or his talk with Jace. His friend was the most grounded individual he knew, other than himself. He might have some insights into Porter's next step.

"Yeah, man. I was just breaking for lunch. Did you bring your tools?"

"I didn't." A jovial smile spread across Sanders face. "I can get them when you run home with me to grab a bite to eat. You know Betha always makes extra for you."

They were as close as family, but Porter sniffed an ulterior motive. "And you can run your inventory needs past me?"

"The furniture you build is legit, dude." Sanders ruffled his sandy blond hair. "I sold a few pieces to a Freemont retailer and they were snapped up. I have your share of the profits."

"Nah." Porter waved away the offer. Sanders and Betha were expecting their first born, they'd have better use for the cash. "Keep supplying me with the raw materials and I'll throw some shit together. It fuels my hobby."

"Betha's not going to let you get away with that."

Sanders was probably right. Like most shifter females, she was a force.

They chatted the entire way through the library. Leaving the building, Porter lifted his face to the warm spring sun. The breeze this time of year still held some of its winter bite, and today it carried a pungent odor. Sanders conversation died away, both males catching sight of the source of the ill smell.

At his work pickup stood Seamus' two favorite henchmen.

Porter hooked his thumbs into his jeans pockets, leveling them with a stare. His eyes were such a dark brown that their near blackness unnerved most people. "Can I help you two ladies?"

Brutus, a male with a neck as thick as his skull, held up a sheet of paper. "I would work on that comedy routine. Cuz you may not be building shit anywhere around here in the near future."

Snatching the paper, Porter tuned out the taunts to read. Sanders peeked over his shoulder. And swore.

No. Fucking. Way. "Why would I be issued a cease and desist?"

"There's been complaints on the quality of your work." Brutus filled in, his tone turning snide.

Porter barely heard, blood pounded too loudly between his ears. "Complaints about what?"

Seamus' other minion, Cletus, smiled, showing broad square teeth. "The roof on the bank addition you completed last month collapsed this morning. Sent two tellers home to heal. Closed the bank until further notice. Seamus was forced to deem your work unsafe and issue the order."

Crinkling the paper and tossing it back to Seamus' lackeys, Porter sneered. "The roof didn't collapse because of me and I can prove it." Porter's expertise would find the bull and the shit of Seamus' claims.

Cletus' jeering grin told Porter that he would have no opportunity to do so. "You've already caused enough emotional trauma to the employees and customers of the bank. Seamus has banned you from the facility until further notice. Considering the trauma it caused, he's been very generous…out of respect for your father, I'm sure."

Porter refused to take the bait; it was wedged in a bear trap. Brutus and Cletus vibrated with anticipation, waiting for him to react. "Thanks, gentlemen. Have a nice day and go fuck yourselves."

Cletus lunged forward, but Brutus yanked him back. "Leave the male alone," he said, in a suspiciously placating manner. "He's just lost his job and now he's stuck here fixing a flat."

Porter's gaze flew to the tires of his truck. The two he could see were normal.

A blade glinted in Cletus' hand as he slammed it into his rear tire.

"Motherfuc—" A promising glare from the knife wielder silenced Porter.

"What's that, Denlan?" Brutus asked. "I don't know if that's the only tire you're having trouble with. I certainly hope your spare is in good condition."

Porter lanced his tongue with a fang to refrain from lobbing more obscenities at the males. Sanders' gaze flew between Porter and the two men. He'd have Porter's back, but the best thing Porter could do for his friend was to keep him out of it.

"That's what I thought." A smug glint passed through Brutus' expression and he focused on Sanders. "How is Betha these days? Doing well?"

Sanders glared back, the threat clearly registered.

Porter's fists clenched, Sanders flexed his fingers, a low growl growing in his chest. The brutes jumped into their ominous white work van and left.

Those vans. They were like reverse animal control units. The animals who needed containment drove the damn things.

If the last three challengers to the leadership position hadn't mysteriously died before the event, Porter would throw the gauntlet down. Unfortunately, he couldn't afford to die by accidental beheading working under his vehicle, be rendered to ash in a house fire, or nick himself with a silver blade and die of silver toxicity like the others. He'd serve his pack best, the whole village, if he outsmarted Seamus.

One name came to mind; his last card to play. It had taken so long to find Jace Stockwell, because he'd grown up as Jace Miller after his mother had ghosted with them. He procrastinated approaching Jace's younger sister because she'd been so young when over half their village had been slaughtered. No more dragging his feet.

It was time for Plan B. B for birthright.

***

Armana Miller scooped two more fudge brownies into the container she was sending home with Maggie. Ma's leftovers. They'd be gone before the end of the night. Those brownies had a shelf life of ten minutes.

"Settle with the chocolate, Ma. That's a lot of stairs I'll need to run."

Her mother dumped in three more. "You can handle it."

Totally. That's why Maggie had egged her on. Her shifter metabolism burned through a nine-by-thirteen pan of gooey goodness in a day. She'd tested it—many times.

Snatching the box, she tucked it under her arm. "I gotta get going. I said I'd help build the new nursery equipment the daycare purchased."

The suspicious expression her mother wore was nothing new. Maggie survived her mother with half-truths. Maybe she could smell it, but Maggie didn't care. She *had* promised, only the furniture arrived Monday, during her shift, and she'd said *if necessary* she could stay late.

It was never necessary, not for baby gear that arrived already assembled.

"Be safe, Maggie," Armana said, giving her a kiss on the cheek.

"Always." Maggie's standard reply.

Armana put human mothers to shame worrying about Maggie. She was nearing the big three-oh, but Ma treated her like an irresponsible teen. And Maggie let her, because all they had were each other. Like Maggie, Armana's friends remained a tail's length away.

"I'm planning pork chops for our Sunday dinner tomorrow night," her mom called as Maggie trotted to her car.

Ah yes. Their standard Sunday dinner. The one day, *every* week, Maggie dedicated to Ma. Yet, Ma called almost every night to ask her over to eat with her. And some mornings for brunch.

If her mom hadn't sworn off their species, Maggie would try to find her a male. Armana attracted human men, ones who'd be a baby compared to her seventy-five years. To a human, Armana looked five or so years older than Maggie, her deep blue eyes bright and sharp, her sable hair always pulled back in a severe bun. Mother and daughter towered over most human women, both five-ten. At this stage in their lives, they pretended to be sisters while in the human world.

Maggie steered into the Kwiki-Mart's parking lot to pull a Superman in the bathroom. Obedient, unadventurous daughter walked into the bathroom, sex in heels walked out. She earned a few double-takes from the customers and employees of the convenience store. The attention more due to her sheer, slinky top providing no coverage for her lacey black bra and tight leather pants than to her change in appearance. Because she was in a hurry, she wore simple red gladiator sandals and pulled her hair back into a high ponytail.

She tossed her clothing in the backseat and tore out of the parking lot, planning her after-shift activities. Her day, up until dinner with her mom, consisted of casing Wally's home. When he'd left to run an errand, she'd broken into the rundown mid-sized home. A quick search through her normal areas of interest—the garbage, the medicine cabinet, and the closet—revealed receipts from two of the popular college hangouts and even a coffee shop, an empty pill bottle, and clothing that smelled of drunk, desperate women.

The desperation wasn't from a girl who couldn't wait to hit it with Wally. Laced with confusion and the sharp bite of despair, the scents were the unique mix of a girl who was helpless to what was happening to her.

How men like Wally continually got away with drugging and raping women, she didn't know. Wait, she did. But unlike the predator who'd torn apart her family, Wally didn't have a ton of money or connections. He had the bland features of a man who blended anywhere, and the knack to pick women who'd be too ashamed or humiliated to seek help. Wally didn't have to plan attacks, he just needed to be in the right spot at the right time. He *orchestrated* the right time. Innocuously drug unsuspecting girls, and if the poor things happened to wander into the parking alone and disoriented, Wally would be there to help.

After Maggie was done with work, the tables were going to be turned on dear Wally.

Chapter Three

Porter followed the little car to a store on the edge of town. He'd hardly ever done more in Freemont than hit the hardware stores and lumber yards, but hunting Jace and his sister had familiarized him with the area. Still, he hadn't heard of The Gift Shop.

He was lucky his mind worked enough to read the words on the sign. With his tire changed, he'd flown to the address he had for Armana Miller in time to see Maggie pull away in her car. He stayed well behind, following her. Parking in an empty lot across from the Kwiki-Mart, he'd almost missed the tall female run into the store. All he saw was long, dark brown hair, and a lush ass filling out blue jeans.

The glimpse was enough for his libido to remind him it'd been awhile. The tensions with Seamus and watching his back had put sex down on the priority list. If a shifter could die during sex, he wouldn't put it past Seamus to figure out how and test it on him.

When Maggie strode out of the convenience store a walking wet dream, he'd felt his blood drain from his brain to his dick. Both screamed for him to go after her, not to let her get away. The entire way to this gift shop place, his head spun and his fangs throbbed to sink into her alabaster skin. He continuously ran his hand through his dark hair in an attempt to calm the dizziness threatening to make him pull over. He'd done it so much, it laid back on his head, no longer falling down on his forehead.

Fantasies of the goddess he'd just seen had distracted him so badly, he'd almost pulled into the parking spot next to her. Forcing himself to park at the dealership next door, he faced the store, anticipating another glimpse of Maggie.

She had just gone inside and all he saw was a closing door.

Blowing out a hard breath, he willed his body down from the sexual precipice before he called into the wind for the beautiful shifter to come and satisfy him.

How was he going to go in and talk with her without a raging hard-on, panting her name?

He'd keep Seamus' evil face in mind at all times. Remember the burial of his father and the three shifters who'd died because they'd displayed a hint of courage.

His dick got the message and calmed the hell down. Porter waited.

What kind of items did this place sell? The shaded windows didn't allow much visual inside the store. Posters that read "Good Vibrations" and "Tasty Samples" hung next to classy lingerie posters. He hadn't heard of a gift shop that sold underwear, but whatever. It's not like he wore any.

The parking lot ebbed and flowed with customers, but only Maggie's car remained the entire time; she must have been the only one working. Porter waited until the lot was empty, hoping to sneak in before the store closed.

At last, it was just Maggie. It was time.

***

Maggie sensed the door opening before the bell dinged. The next customer's scent hit her nose, flipped her stomach, and started a warm glow deep in the area of her body that most of the store's toys catered to.

What the hell?

The fact that the next customer was a shifter registered as her eyes landed on him.

He swaggered in, his swarthy bemused expression scanning the interior. A lock of cocoa brown hair fell over his forehead, the rest pushed back off his face. He wore a red plaid shirt that hung open over a white tee molded to an extremely cut torso.

Gawd. Pecs and abs beckoned her attention, but the low hanging carpenter jeans promised the ridges of muscle that she wanted to rim with her tongue down to the juncture between his—

"Mage Troye?"

Ripped from her dreamy contemplation of the hot shifter stranger, she frowned in confusion. "Sorry?"

"You're Maggie Miller?"

Straightening from the counter, she switched from *swept away by the hot shifter* to *who the fuck is he and why does he know my name?* "Maybe."

"Then you're also Mage Troye, your given name. I need to talk to you."

"I've never heard of Mage Troye," *Who named their kid Mage? What did he think her middle name was? Witch?* "and I don't need to talk to you. If you're not here to shop, you need to leave." Her heart whimpered at the idea he might go.

Great. So she was crazy—or this guy was.

"Lobo Springs needs your help."

Now, Lobo Springs rang a bell; a faint one. She remembered her mother and Jace arguing about the place. The only reason she remembered was because when she'd later asked her mom where "Loco Springs" was, her mom's face lost color and she demanded Maggie never speak of the town again.

"Lobo Springs," the hot shifter prompted, "your home."

"I've lived in Freemont as long as I can remember. I'm not the girl you're looking for."

His hooded eyes drifted down her body suggesting she was a girl, and he was definitely okay with finding her.

~34~

She really hoped the gauzy shirt she wore over her bra hid her peaked nipples because she'd hate to waste the effort of masking her sexual interest only to have it on full display.

Stalking toward the counter, he spoke low. "Your mom took you away after the attack that killed your father and brother. Your father, Bane, was our leader, Keve his heir. I've already talked to Jace and he—"

She cut a hand through the air to silence him. "Wait. You spoke to Jace? When? Where?"

The shifter gave her a sidelong look. "Several months ago. At Pale Moonlight."

She'd heard of the club. No humans knew it was a shifter club, but its loose reputation made it popular with the crowd looking to score. Males and females flocked there on the weekends to find out how many orgasms could kill them. Maggie had never been there, but maybe she should plan a visit, especially if this dude hung out there.

"Yeah, and what'd he say?" Her question held an air of nonchalance, not like she was hanging on the guy's every word that he'd seen her brother.

A calculating gleam entered his deep chocolate eyes. "If I tell you, will you let me tell you why I'm here?"

He smelled her eagerness. Hopefully, just about information about her brother, and not regarding her body's reaction to him.

"You tell me about Jace first."

The side of his mouth—that sensual, full mouth—twitched. "As I was saying, I talked to your brother and he refused to come back and claim his birthright of leading the village. He's dedicated to his position as a Guardian and doesn't want to put his human mate's life in danger."

Jace was mated.

Tears threatened to well. She wasn't even sure he'd gotten out of jail. Suspected he wouldn't want anything to do with her since she was the reason he was incarcerated. Her mother had driven him away, and he continued life without them.

Regret was a dish best served by herself. She and her mother were truly alone. Her little girl fantasies that her brother would come back and just be a brother shattered.

"So," Maggie cleared her throat to keep from choking up, "he's a Guardian?" *What's a Guardian?*

The male's gaze softened. "When's the last time you talked to him?"

"Been awhile," she hedged. "Anyway, you were saying? Lobo Springs?"

"The male who won the fight for leadership is an evil bastard, destroying our village slowly year by year."

"If he's destroying the village, then there wouldn't be anything left for him to rule."

He blinked. And blinked again. "By destroying, I mean he's slowly taking control of our assets, our finances, and anyone who disagrees with him."

"And then what?"

His mouth quirked again. "And then he has total control, his pick of the females who won't have a choice, and no one will know better because he's technologically controlled the village so effectively, no one could leave if they wanted to." She opened her mouth, but he held up a finger, shushing her. "Let me finish, there's another customer coming in."

Of course there was. It was almost closing time.

"The TriSpecies Synod passed a law to let the clans of each colony vote in their leadership as a way to integrate them into the new world. Seamus has intimidated everyone into agreeing to let him remain head of Lobo Springs." He took a deep breath, pinning her with his unnerving, engaging stare. "But if a Troye were to come back and claim birthright, Lobo Springs would be theirs by blood. Seamus wouldn't have a say."

The door dinged announcing another customer and Hot Shifter stepped back, pretending to browse the shelves. Good luck with that. The section he was in catered to the BDSM crowd.

There was so much disturbing about what he said. He thought she was Mage Troye. Her mom had only ever called her Maggie, which meant her name was just Maggie, or her mom had been very careful. Porter had tracked Jace down, who would've been old enough to remember another name, but she'd been so young. Too little for clear memories.

When he talked about the shifter world, she didn't know what the hell he was saying. Guardian? TriSpecies Synod? Clans and colonies and birthrights, it was all second semester Latin to her. The class she'd failed. And wouldn't Seamus just kill her if he was as awful as Porter claimed?

The late arrivals were two girls giggling in the lube aisle. Maggie wandered over to them in hopes to get them moving. She needed to close the store and track down Wally.

"Can I help you ladies with anything?"

Hot Shifter meandered away from the whips and cuffs section looking a little bewildered. The girls noticed him, eyes tracking him the whole way. The wild part of Maggie didn't like that. The wolf in her wanted to pick them each up by the scruff of the neck and haul their Zumba'd asses out. Then she'd go take her aggression out on Wally the pervert because she hated feeling…territorial?

"We were just deciding which one to get." One girl answered. Maggie was surprised they'd even noticed her presence. Hot Shifter dominated the room, and their attention. "Um, what do you recommend?"

"Is it for you or him? There's flavored lube and flavored condoms."

"Him," both replied in unison. Hot Shifter disappeared into the X-rated video room.

Maggie snickered before turning her attention back to the women. "I'd go with a condom. It's got the normal plasticy undertones, but a pleasing flavor overall, and they catch the mess so you don't have to. I think strawberries and cream is the most popular flavor, but we do carry a variety pack."

The women each snagged a variety box. When they left, Maggie locked the door, shutting her in with the stranger. Hot Shifter didn't smell like a danger to her. Physically at least.

He ambled into view when he heard the door shutting.

"So what's your name, anyway?" She feared she'd accidently call him Hot Shifter.

"Porter Denlan." The low timbre of his voice stroked her every nerve ending.

Maggie changed her mind. He was physically dangerous. "The store's closed. You need to leave."

"*We* need to talk."

"Um, no, Mr. Denlan. We don't." She hated to drive him away, but what he asked of her was ridiculous. "Let me lay it out straight. I was raised human. Mage Troye, she doesn't exist." Determination poured from her. Continuing to argue with her was futile, and he needed to realize that.

Porter's nostrils flared, his gaze hardened. "Many of us in the village strongly suspect he's behind the deaths of three shifters who talked of challenging him to become leader. If Seamus is allowed to continue, he'll only get more blatant. You're going to allow a lot of innocent shifters to get killed."

Ouch, that one hit her weak spot. Protecting young women from people like Wally called to her. Working at the daycare didn't suit her, but she was ferociously protective of the kids. The idea her inaction threatened innocents unsettled her. Yet, following Porter because he insisted she was the answer was foolish. "And how would *I* not end up getting killed?"

"The village would back your claim because it'd take the pressure off of them. And I'd be there to protect you."

She scoffed at his offer of protection. He waltzed into her work and claimed she must go back to a village to save people, who may or may not accept her, *if* what he said was true. Then he didn't quite come out and say there was danger involved, but alluded to shifters perishing at Seamus' hand, the guy she was supposed to challenge, and he offered protection. Him, an unarmed dude looking like he just walked off a construction site.

Crossing her arms, she studied his appearance. "Are those paint smears? Is your weapon a paint brush?"

His jaw flexed before he answered. "It's mud."

"White mud?"

"To seam sheetrock." He answered as if, duh, wasn't it obvious?

"So you what, work in construction? And your weapon of choice is a saw? Hammer?" Who said bitchiness wasn't a great defensive tactic? What he asked of her plucked all of her inadequate shifter insecurities. Like how she knew she was different from everyone around her, but understood next to nothing about how her people lived. Call it her gut, intuition, but she wasn't the one meant to rescue Lobo Springs. "You need to leave, Porter. My answer is no."

He approached. She refused to back up. The closer he got, the more her body urged her to meet him, press into his strong frame. Tilting her head back as he towered over her, she wished she wore her heels. Then he'd only have a couple of inches advantage.

"Do you really want me to leave?" He spoke softly, heat radiating off his body, warming hers in the right places.

She drew in a deliberate breath, licked her lips, instantly regretting the movement. His eyes zeroed in on her lips, pupils dilated, his breaths slow, intentional. He was controlling his own body's reaction as carefully as she was.

Did she really want him to leave? Her pebbled nipples, tingling core, and raging hormones screamed *no*. "Yes." She exhaled, the word requiring more effort than she'd put into speech her entire life.

Disbelief lightened his expression. He peered down at her, drifted an inch closer.

Hastily, she stepped back. Hurt and confusion permeated the air.

"If you were raised by humans," he said, "what do you know about shifters?"

She shuttered her expression, hoping to hide her lack of knowledge. "I know enough."

He coughed out a laugh. "I doubt that. I'll give you time, Maggie. But I'll be back. I promise you that."

Her gauzy shirt rippled as a shiver whispered through her. Porter snatched the keys from her hand, marched to the door, and unlocked it to let himself out, leaving the keys in the deadbolt.

Exiting Porter was just as mouth-watering as Entering Porter. Those baggy pants couldn't hide an ass like that. Each step adjusted the thick material enough to tease her with hints of muscular thighs. Nothing could make her glance away. She remained mesmerized until he drove away.

How could she not have followed anything Porter said about their people? Muscle memory saved her while closing the store. Her body felt like an empty conch shell—the warm life that had once resided inside was gone, leaving an echoing cavern. Three times she counted the cash register because she'd drifted off, Porter filling her thoughts, leaving her a little less bereft, until she forced herself back to awareness.

So much precious night had been wasted on her scattered thoughts and old regrets. She needed to shake it off. Hunting Wally should do the trick.

Chapter Four

Porter drove down the street and parked, keeping a close eye on the store and Maggie.

His mind was scrambled after his encounter with the gorgeous shifter.

Raised human.

What the hell had Armana Troye—Miller—whatever she called herself these days—been thinking?

Raised as a human.

Was that why she acted like she didn't know who he was to her. Didn't give a rat's furry behind about what happened to his home, to the shifters there. He'd built half that town. After the attacks, he utilized what his father had taught him and, board by board, rebuilt what had been taken from them.

And Maggie had no interest in returning to save it all.

She wasn't totally clueless about their connection. He affected her. Not with anger, not with fear, but with pure lust. She'd wanted him and wouldn't admit it—to him or herself.

Jace had been completely tight-lipped about his family. Porter wouldn't have guessed they were estranged, and he wanted to know why. Hell, he wanted to learn everything about the knockout in the strappy red sandals, body-hugging clothing, and dominatrix ponytail.

Sex shop, he snorted. He'd been bombarded by her sex appeal and surrounded by erotic images. Yeah, they might've been tasteful, but they filled a male's mind with ideas. Like how blue her eyes would be wearing nothing but skin and that pale pink collar he saw hanging in a display, her breasts pushed up high by…nothing. He instinctively knew they'd defy gravity.

Groaning against the pressure in his pants, he shifted, seeking relief. Nothing short of driving into Maggie's sultry body, savoring the dampness he scented on her encompassing his cock, would help him feel less strung out.

She was perfect. Not just for him, but for the colony. He sensed strength and more than a dose of stubbornness. With his help, she'd develop into a fine leader.

No, he wasn't giving up on Maggie Miller.

And where was the object of his surveillance going?

He didn't follow her immediately, wanted to remain hidden as he trailed her through town. There wasn't much traffic this time of night which made it both easier and harder to remain undetected. He circled around the block to avoid getting too close and still be able to distinguish her headlights when he returned to the proper road.

After one go-round, he worried he'd truly lost her only to notice her car creeping through a popular club's parking lot. He waited until she exited and resumed tailing her.

She did that two more times before parking down the street from the fourth club.

Either she was really picky on venues or she searched for someone.

Contemplating that someone being male summoned a deep rage Porter hadn't known existed within himself. He was the calm one, possessed a rare level head found in male shifters. She had asked if his weapon was a saw or hammer. No, if she sought male company after meeting him, the only weapons he needed were his hands and fangs.

Except she remained in her car.

Young men and women staggered randomly out of the club. Some left individually, a few in groups. His keen eyes picked up a young girl weaving into the parking lot. She dropped her keys, almost fell picking them up, walked a couple more steps, dropping her keys again.

Sweet Mother, she wasn't thinking about driving was she?

Humans and their liquor.

Then Porter noticed an average-looking male running up to help her. And Maggie was heading toward the couple.

Porter frowned. She was wearing a dark hooded sweatshirt with the hood up. A pair of Nikes replaced the sexy sandals. She wasn't wearing that when she left the store; she had to have changed while driving. He regretted having to keep his distance.

The man assisted the girl to her car, helping her into the backseat. Maggie broke into a run, slamming him into the door, using his body to shut it.

Porter jumped out, rushing to the scuffle.

A sickening thud rang through the night. The guy's head rebounded off the car. He tried struggling, but was no match against another species. Maggie dragged him off the car and slammed him to the ground. She waited until he tried to rise to aim her boot for a kidney shot.

Porter winced; the man groaned. He scanned the parking lot, but Maggie had moved fast and efficiently. Her and the male were hidden between two vehicles.

"What the hell are you doing?" Porter skidded to a halt behind Maggie.

Her head whipped around. "I don't believe it," she hissed.

Looking into the car, he saw the young girl in a passed out heap across the seat.

"He was going to rape her," Maggie answered.

Porter jerked his attention back to Maggie who held the man down, stuffing a rag into his mouth. "And you know this how?"

Yanking the man's head up, she firmly gripped his hair. "I'm right, aren't I?"

He tried shaking his head, but Maggie reached deep between his legs, grabbing a fistful of man junk. "He hunts them, searching for the ones who are alone. After he slips something into their drink, he waits for them to decide they don't feel good and need to go home. Then he abuses them and they rarely remember. If they do, they have nothing to tell the cops."

She squeezed her hand and twisted. The guy squealed. Porter closed his stance like he needed to protect his own package.

Leaning down, she twisted his hair in her fist, whispering in his ear. "Guess you're not getting away with this one."

A snap of her other fist into his temple and he hung limp.

Porter stood, dumbfounded. His protective instincts held him in place, masking her so passersby didn't witness her violence.

Maggie pulled out the man's phone and dialed 9-1-1, leaving the phone open, not answering the dispatcher's questions. She ripped open his shirt and produced a black marker from her hoodie.

"What are you doing?" Porter exclaimed. He hadn't sensed crazy from her, but he didn't know how else to categorize what he'd just seen.

She threw him a dirty look over her shoulder. "Why'd you follow me?"

"I wanted to make sure you got home okay." Not a total lie.

Speaking around the marker cap she held between her teeth, she said, "I will once you go away."

She scrawled "I drug girls and rape them" over the man's chest.

Succinct.

"Not a chance. I gotta hear this story." Her precise, determined scrawls…he believed the guy had done exactly what she wrote.

"It's none of your business."

Maggie opened the car door and checked on the girl's breathing before closing her back in. Sirens sounded in the distance.

"That's my cue to get out of here." She pulled her hood farther down and trotted back to her car.

He kept pace. "How many times have you done this and what about the cameras?"

"I repeat, none of your business. As for the cameras, they're pretty sketchy. Details are hard to read. All they know is two dudes jumped the pervert and beat him until police arrived. The police will half-heartedly investigate because they'll discover much more interesting evidence on Wally Donaldson."

"No way anyone's going to believe you're male. If your sweater covered your ass, maybe, but your thighs inspire men to think about...things..."

Maggie's step stalled when she caught the meaning behind his words. She recovered, apparently unconcerned about her disguise epically failing. "It won't matter."

She jumped in the driver's seat and pulled away. He stood, waiting. When her eyes flicked up to the rearview mirror, he grinned and waved. The engine roared as she stepped on the gas.

If Maggie thought she was getting away that easily...

Porter ran to his car, and like before, he tailed her home.

***

Her thighs inspired him. Maggie harrumphed. Her thighs.

She wasn't dying to know if they conjured the same passionate images in him as his hard body in those loose carpenter jeans did for her. She wasn't.

Just like she wasn't parked in her spot at her apartment building, staring at the steering wheel, pondering what Porter imagined her thighs doing to him.

Enough of this!

Grabbing her clothing, she climbed out and headed for the stairwell.

And stopped.

She sniffed.

Shifters. Male.

Not Porter. Where his scent curled around her belly, igniting a fire in her nether region she'd never experienced, this scent robbed her of heat. Filled her with dread—and fear.

The underground parking garage set up the perfect environment for hiding. She'd never worried before. All the complex's occupants were human. Very few humans overpowered a shifter, even one who literally didn't know her own strength.

The stairwell door flew open and a hulking form barreled out—straight for her.

Maggie tossed her armload in his face and kicked out. Her foot nailed his abdomen, earning her a grunt from the giant male. His forward momentum continued, but she danced out of his way…into another solid body.

Instinct snapped her elbow up into the male's face. He sputtered and gagged; he was so tall, she'd nailed his Adam's apple.

The first assailant landed a blow to her stomach. She cried out, but couldn't double over because, despite her brutal hit, the second giant held her ponytail in his steel trap of a grip.

"Signal Dugger to bring the van around."

Maggie's organs throbbed. How large was that male's fist? She writhed, thrashed, screeched. A hand clamped over her mouth and she took great pleasure in biting a finger to the bone, blood pooling in her mouth.

"You bitch!" The hulk shoved her into the other goliath who grabbed her by the forearms. Maggie sprayed him with her mouthful of blood.

He yanked her close to rasp in her ear. "You'll regret that." He stiffened, as if suddenly aware of something. She used the opening to fight with every muscle fiber she had. It did no good. He was giant.

The shifter with the ravaged digit stilled. "Denlan."

With a sudden spike of hope, she sensed him, too. A barreling force of rage shoved into the man holding Maggie captive, throwing them both forward several feet. She fell free and rolled away.

Wrestling between the two giant shifters was a flurry of sheetrock mud-stained clothing.

She never thought she'd be grateful the insistent male followed her. As ferociously as he fought, he was outnumbered, wasn't going to last long against the two shifters. As broad and cut as his body was, he was outmuscled.

Maggie waited, prepared to make her move. Porter ripped off one assailant, who stumbled back.

She jumped behind him and slammed her hands on each side of his head, a brutal double blow to his sensitive shifter ears. He yelled out, throwing his hands to his head, but she jerked him back, using the same move she'd used on Wally.

Head met car frame.

Unlike with Wally, she used her full strength. A knock on the head won't kill her kind. The shifter slumped against the window and slid to the ground. Maggie stomped him in the face—just to be thorough.

Porter sat astride the second assailant, fists wailing, getting bucked around like he was on a prizewinning bull. The other shifter was too brawny for Porter to knock him out before he was overpowered.

Maggie raced behind Porter, placing a well-aimed kick on the prone male's testicles.

The howl of agony straight from a werewolf horror movie ricocheted off the concrete walls. Porter hugged both arms around the male's thick neck and yanked to the side. Bone-cracking gave way to spooky silence, except for Maggie's jagged breathing.

Ohmigod, ohmigod, ohmigod. Two bodies sprawled like they were dead. Their heads were still attached; they'd heal.

Porter jumped up and grabbed her arm, dragging her behind him. "They were sent by Seamus."

She pulled against him. "There's a…a Dugger somewhere still around."

"Not anymore," Porter said grimly.

"Oh. Okay…Did you kill him?" Would she care?

In the dim lighting, Porter's masculine, harsh features appeared deadlier than the two hulks who attacked her. Hulk Squared. Or would it be cubed? She hadn't the pleasure of meeting Dugger.

"No, but all three of them deserve it. I recognized the van from Seamus' team. He didn't notice me until I punched through the window and clobbered him. You were correct about my weapons. A hammer worked just fine." Porter's triumphant snicker…turned her on. Now was not the time.

Porter dragged her out into the night. A white van with a shattered driver's window idled in front of the closed garage doors. Dugger spilled into the passenger seat, a thick shoulder visible above the window. Porter reached in and grabbed his trusty hammer. His beat-up single cab pickup was parked down the street, and they quickly made their way to it.

"What did they want with me?"

"To kill you, probably."

She squeezed his hand tighter, the news of a kill order out on her stifled her fierce independence. Wally had nothing on even one of her three attackers. Porter stroked her palm with his thumb. It was both reassuring and sensual. She didn't want him to stop.

"Shouldn't we behead them or something?" Maggie hopped into the passenger seat and locked the door as soon as Porter shut it behind her.

Killing a living, breathing body while it lay unconscious did not sit well with her code of ethics. But getting chased by three Hulks was not what she wanted to experience. Then there were her instincts screaming at her to do *something* to keep them from attacking another innocent again. She knew the feeling well; it propelled her after sexual predators like Wally.

Porter slid into his seat, draped an arm over the wheel, and faced her. "Have you ever killed anyone before, Maggie?"

She shook her head.

"Even if we could behead them and load their dead bulk into their van before any one of them regains consciousness, it'd be difficult to do without being noticed." He punched the truck into drive and sped away. "And I don't care to have a price on my head. Killing three shifters from Seamus' pack would be more than enough reason for him to justifiably be rid of me—and be the hero for it."

"What's the whole colony-clan thing? Is Lobo Springs a clan or a colony?"

Porter took his attention off the road to gape at her. "You really were raised human."

She rolled her eyes at him. "That's why I said it."

Porter maneuvered through traffic until he found a quiet street and parked. He turned to face her. "What do you know about shifters?"

Embarrassingly little, and Maggie had hoped to avoid revealing her lack of knowledge of her own species. "We're stronger, faster, our senses are acute. We can be killed by beheading, burning, or silver, otherwise we can live centuries."

Maggie's mom was already making plans for them to move, fretted they had stayed too long. Since money didn't grow on the lilac bushes in her mom's backyard, it was easier said than done. Maggie couldn't claim to be helpful. She didn't want to leave.

His dark gaze bored into her. "Anything else?"

Lost in his captivating eyes, she blinked. If he was searching for more, he was only going to be disappointed.

His voice dropped an octave. "What do you feel around me, Maggie?"

"Forward much?" she huffed. Like she was going to tell him that the word horny was an understatement as soon as she'd met him. "I only met you a few hours ago; why would I feel anything?"

Laugh lines that didn't get much use crinkled with smugness. "It'd only take a second to know." He leaned across the console. "Tell me what you felt when I walked into the store."

She should cringe back against the window, but to her horror she drifted toward him, mesmerized by his lips. They were moving, but she didn't hear him. Blood pounded between her ears, screaming "kiss me!"

Then three words broke through the din. "You're my mate."

Maggie reared back, knocking her head on the passenger window. "Ouch! What?"

Porter chuckled ruefully. He was one of the lucky ones to find his mate so early. At only fifty-four, he was quite young in shifter years. Maggie sat next to him, proof that going feral from a lack of the mating bond wasn't in his future. He wasn't going to turn into Seamus, calculating and cruel.

"Mate?" She sputtered, shaking her head like he was insane.

"You felt it. If I did, you did."

"And then what? I'm supposed to rush off and marry you because you said we belong together?"

Fuuuck. The urge to shake Armana was unrelenting. She was Maggie's only connection to their world, and she'd failed to school Maggie on any of it.

"Yes," he said, evenly. "Shifters don't marry. Mating is so much deeper."

He stopped at Maggie's snigger. "I'll bet. *Deeper.*"

His pupils must've flared at the image she conjured for him because she fell silent.

"Shifters can go crazy and die if they don't meet their mates. We call it going feral. Our mates are our world. Without them we cannot live." He let his words sink in.

"I'm not in the mating mood."

He leisurely inhaled and cocked a brow. Her face flushed red.

"You know what I mean. I'm not thinking about mating, or anything else," she shot him a pointed glare, "until I'm not being hunted."

Fine. If she wanted to avoid the mating topic, he'd let it drop. Porter studied his mate. "I have no idea what Armana was thinking when she took off with you, when she failed to teach you our ways."

If Maggie had been in her wolf form, her hackles would've raised. "She was thinking of keeping her surviving son and daughter alive."

"Ignorance does not protect."

"Says the male here asking for *my* help, the girl who was raised human."

Touché. He pulled back into traffic, heading nowhere, but a moving target was harder to hit. "Did Armana at least teach you that females respect their males, obeying them explicitly?"

"Now I know you're full of shit. There's no way Ma was a good little housewife." Her voice held more than a touch of fondness.

He couldn't help but smile, something he seemed to do frequently around her. "I'm joking, but only about that. To answer your question, packs are like families that make up clans; clans form a colony. It was basically whoever could get along together built their houses around each other, forming a town. Lobo Springs has six clans. A small town among human standards, but a sizeable congregation of shifters."

Maggie nodded as if she'd think about it later and switched topics. "Where are we going?"

"To find a place to catch some sleep." The adrenaline rush from discovering Dugger to Maggie's attempted abduction had faded. The previous day had been long and tiring: his profession and friend threatened, fixing his tire, tracking down Maggie. She was in his truck, safe for now, and he wanted only to curl up with her. Not that she'd allow it judging from her reaction to the news she belonged to him.

Maggie gasped, looking around. "My purse! Do you have a phone? I need to call Ma. I'll give you the address, you need to head there."

"Sorry, Maggie. If they found you, they know where she is and could be waiting for us." He tossed her his phone. "Call and warn her, but we can't go over there."

Maggie stared blankly at the phone. He sensed her worry. She keyed in her mom's number, and waited tensely.

"Ma," her relief was palpable. "Listen, some shifters tried to kidnap me. You need to find somewhere else to stay for a while."

Porter picked up her mom's calm words. "Tell me everything."

Had she been expecting it, thought it was inevitable Maggie would get dragged back into their world? Or was she a cool duck under pressure, like her daughter?

"Three huge shifters were waiting for me at home after work." Interesting. Did Armana not know about Maggie's extracurricular vigilante activities? "No, we didn't kill them."

"We?" Armana picked up on that right away.

"Denlan. Porter Denlan helped me fight them off, says they're from Lobo Springs."

There was silence on the other end before her mom acquiesced. "The Denlans were a good pack, came from a good clan."

"Ma?" Maggie glanced at him, then tilted her head down, like it would keep him from hearing her next words. "He says he's my mate."

More silence. Served Armana right for keeping her daughter in the dark.

"Go with your gut, Maggie."

Go with your gut? She keeps Maggie's biology and birthright from her and then says *that*? What the fuck?

"Be safe, Ma."

"I got away once, I'll get away again. Maggie…stay away from Lobo Springs. Only death waits for you there."

"Armana," Porter raised his voice so she heard him clearly, "Jace is with the West Creek Guardians. Go find him and start talking." Especially about why she fled. Her ominous warning to Maggie suggested it was more than from losing her mate and child and being in mourning.

"Jace is a Guardian?" Armana sounded stunned...and proud.

"West Creek is just across the river." Maggie held the phone out so they could have a shifter conference call. "Even if they follow you, these Guardians won't allow them to hurt you, would they?"

No, but if Porter was Jace, he might let them.

"I will go. Denlan." Armana barked, her voice full of authority. "You will take my daughter there."

"Lobo Springs needs her, Armana. Your sudden departure left the colony open to a hostile takeover."

"Um, she is here, and is an adult." Irritation from Maggie filled the cab. "I'll make my own decisions from now on, do you both understand?"

"Maggie," Armana pleaded, "please find the Guardians. They will protect you."

"I've been *overprotected* my whole life," Maggie muttered. "I'll call when I make my decision, Ma. Now run. Please."

"Very well. Be safe."

***

Armana disconnected, looking forlornly at the phone. She'd given up *everything* to keep them safe and it wasn't enough.

She looked around the house she had scrimped and saved for while knowing eventually she'd have to leave. Human acquaintances she'd known for years already marveled over how youthful she looked.

She'd stalled too long and the past caught up with her daughter.

Jace was a Guardian?

How he must hate her. Armana hated herself for the way she'd had to treat him after he went to prison. Jace had a right to know the truth about why.

The Guardians could help her family. It's why she'd stayed in Freemont regardless of its proximity to Lobo Springs. Big enough to get lost in, but with an honorable Guardian pack nearby if she ever needed help. That, and she'd had no funds to carry her farther with two small children.

She didn't need help, but Maggie did. And she owed Jace after what she'd done to him.

Armana moved around her tiny house, pulling curtains shut like she did every night. Maggie always teased her about her fastidious nature, but what her daughter didn't know was that it was for survival. She'd never had enough money to run far from Seamus, so her only option had been to completely remove her family from shifter life.

Some might condemn her decision, but they were welcome to find themselves in the same tight spot and see what they'd do.

Porter Denlan. She'd heard the derision in his voice. Her memory of every shifter in what was then called Great Moon remained clear as a bell. The last night there was branded in her brain, like the image of a young Porter draped over his bloodied mother. He'd always been a good kid. She wondered how he'd changed since the attack.

Her daughter's mate.

Armana sighed. She had wished fervently that Maggie wouldn't run across her mate for several decades, and more importantly that he wasn't anyone from Lobo Springs.

Sweet Mother, what a mess.

She threw clothing into a bag and tossed a few toiletries on top. Unless the West Creek Guardians had moved, she knew approximately where their pack resided. And if Porter wanted what was best for Maggie, he'd bring her there immediately.

But Armana had another stop to make first.

Chapter Five

Maggie fumed. Porter thought he was calling the shots and wanted to drag her to a colony she didn't remember for a non-hostile, but maybe a little violent, takeover. Her mother apparently had a helluva secret to tell and wanted Maggie to run to the Guardians.

And she didn't even know who they were!

"What exactly are the Guardians?"

Porter's brows shot up before he shook his head, flabbergasted at her lack of knowledge.

"For fuck's sake, is it a big deal that I don't know all this? I mean I was doing just fine until the Loco Springs crew showed up."

Yeah, she'd messed up the name on purpose, and it vexed him so. She made a note to do it more often.

"Guardians are the police force for our kind. The Lycan and Vampire Councils were dismantled last year, and our new government, the TriSpecies Synod, integrated shifters and vampires."

"Tri? What's the third species?"

"Hybrids."

Shifters and vampires got it on? Maggie sighed.

Overall, it sounded easy enough to understand. Had to be better than learning about the branches of the US government in school. The biggest bonus was that Porter smelled much better than sitting among a mass of smells-likes-teen-spirit with her superior sense of smell. "Was that momentous?"

"Yeeahh, you could say that."

Maggie wanted to be offended, she really did, but she made the mistake of looking at him. Running a hand through his dark hair to sweep it off his forehead, his other arm draped across the steering wheel, accentuating his broad shoulders and lean torso, he jacked up her insides. Her girl parts weren't confused or in turmoil; they were demanding to have the male next to her.

To her mortification, he could probably smell it.

Why couldn't she detect sexual frustration on him?

He set his elbow by the window, resting his head in his hand, streetlights flashing across his stark features. All she sensed from him was trepidation and resolve.

Maggie's desire was going to clog the cab of his truck if she couldn't get herself under control.

"Have you been estranged from Jace?"

"Yeeahh, you could say that." *How does it feel, jackass?* Instead of being affronted, his lips quirked, and it sucked the fun right of her sarcastic remark.

She sighed and committed herself to the words spilling from her, as if it would be enough for anyone to understand how she'd abandoned her kin. "Was it wrong? Yes. But I was afraid I'd lose Ma if I associated with my own brother." Chalk another note up on her guilt board.

"What'd he do?"

No one else knew but her, Jace, and her mother, and possibly Jace's mate, who probably despised them by default. Before there'd been no one she could talk to about the whole situation, or her life, really. The attack back at her apartment, Porter jumping in, something shifted between them. Perhaps just in her, but for once, she was going to admit to the reason behind her fractured relationship with her brother. "Saved my life."

Baffled, Porter ripped his eyes off the road to meet hers.

"Yep. I was working at an old diner and this creepy guy kept hanging out around closing time. Jace usually gave me a ride home. One day he was late. We locked the diner, and I was stuck outside waiting for him. Creepy guy jumped me."

Maggie rested her head back on the seat. She should ask where they were going, but right now she didn't care. Their conversation was cathartic, and the shameful part hadn't yet been spoken. How Porter would react, she didn't know, but the tiny space within the cab, with him, felt safe.

"He was a big shot. Rich. Connections. Jace hunted him down before I was hurt. Beat the shit out of him."

"Good." Porter's jaw flexed, looking like he'd hunt the pervert down to whip him again.

"In the struggle, a nightstand got knocked over and…" Maggie shuddered at the memory. "All these pictures of the girls he abused before me spilled out. Jace made the ultimate decision to rid the world of his filth."

"Good," Porter repeated.

"For the world. Not for Jace. Raised poor, dressed like a thug, he was eaten alive in court. Brought too much attention to us and Ma quit anything to do with Jace. Ordered me to do the same."

And the shame had eaten her alive ever since.

For the first time since she'd met him, she wished Porter would say something. Was he regretting who fate paired him with? From his appearance, he'd dropped everything to rush to Freemont for her, only to find out she wasn't a shifter in shining armor. If she turned her back on her family, why in the world would he continue to recruit her to save a whole village?

"That explains your weekend fun."

Maggie sputtered, then laughed. "It's effective therapy for feeling like a worthless pansy for turning my back on Jace."

Porter's smile died. "He's mated to a human. The Guardians recruited him. He did okay for himself."

Maggie smiled sadly. "Because he's a good guy."

"Guardians are born; we know them by scent. Promising shifters can be recruited, only with good reason. He protected you and your mom. Wouldn't tell me where you were, never gave me any indication you were estranged. Didn't even tell me he'd changed his name from Miller to Stockwell when he was mated."

Aww, she'd always known he was an honorable male. His sinister features invited negative impressions from strangers, but Maggie hadn't experienced anything from him but respect and caring. Stockwell sounded like a good name. She wasn't particularly attached to Miller, either. Troye wasn't really an option, even if it must be her real name. "Mage Troye, huh? Did you know me?"

"I knew your family, of course, who you were, but no, I was just a little older then than you are now."

"That's so weird."

"Not for us. You'll get used to the way we live."

Uh, no, she wouldn't. She was just fine living the way she was. That was a lie she wouldn't get away with; she was repressed and unfulfilled.

They pulled into the lot of a cheap chain motel. Maggie was tired, vacillated between running forever and finding her brother, but spending the night in the same room with Porter wasn't on her list of options.

"I'm not staying here with you."

Porter found a parking spot and killed the engine. "We're not staying here." At her questioning look, he pointed behind them to another low budget motel. "We're staying there. Then tomorrow morning, we're finding another set of wheels because they'll be looking for my truck."

He had a point and a decent plan...that still involved her sleeping in the same room as him. "I'm not going to Lobo Springs."

"We'll talk in the room."

He climbed out, seemingly unfazed by the prospect of sleeping close to her. Attempting rest in the same room as a sexy carpenter certainly rattled her.

***

"One queen-sized bed, please."

Porter ignored the jab in his shins and the glare from a stunning set of pale blue eyes.

He paid in cash, grabbed the key, and flashed her a wolfish grin.

She rounded on him as soon as they entered their room. "What were you thinking?"

"I was thinking it was cheaper. Do you have any cash on you?" Porter had more than enough, but she didn't have to know that.

She pursed her lips and crossed her arms, eyeing the bed dubiously. "I can go to the bank tomorrow."

"Not on a Sunday. You can use the bathroom first. I'm going to comb the yellow pages looking for a car rental place that's open tomorrow."

Maggie stomped into the bathroom and Porter bit back a laugh. She was afraid she'd give in to her urges around him. He'd been fighting them all night to keep from pulling into a secluded spot and discovering how long it would take to pull down her tight pants.

They were mates and now she knew it. What she didn't know was how dedicated to each other mates were. Porter planned to use it against her. Her insistence that Lobo Springs meant nothing to her ratcheted up his determination to get her there. If she stepped foot in the place of her birth, it'd settle into her bones, she'd attach to the people. Then she wouldn't be able to leave it to Seamus' mercy.

Maggie sauntered out of the bathroom, completely dressed, but her shiny hair hung down her back. His fingers itched to bury themselves in it. He'd built a mahogany cabinet once out of aged wood that had developed into a deep, rich brown like her hair. How fitting he'd describe her hair like that.

Kicking off her shoes, she toed them next to the bed and crawled between the covers.

Settle in sweetheart. Porter took his turn in the bathroom, neatly hanging up his pants and shirt on the door hook. When he was done, the lights were off. Not an issue for a shifter, just a signal from Maggie that she only planned on sleeping.

Her still form curled in the blankets, facing the wall, was another signal. One Porter planned to ignore. He settled in next to her.

Maggie twisted to peer at him, her eyes opening wide at his nudity. "What are you doing? Where are your clothes?"

He reclined on his back, his arms behind his head. "Resting, and hanging up in the bathroom."

"So you just thought you'd slide into bed naked?"

"We're open with our bodies. It's not like we can have someone waiting with a robe when we shift to our wolf and back."

"I can't sleep with you like that. There's a chair for you."

A tiny leather one offering no more room than a folding chair. "I don't think so, beautiful."

"Then *I'll* sleep there."

She threw the sheets back, but Porter grabbed her arm, rolling her under him, anchoring her arms above her head. She gasped, shocked he moved so quickly. Gulping she looked around as if noticing for the first time she was on her back, he stretched over her, and she was pinned.

"We're both adults, Maggie. What are you afraid of?"

She strained against his grip, her pelvis pushing up against his groin. Felt so good. His erection free of any restraints. The raspy material of her jeans exquisite agony against his tender flesh.

"Are you worried that I'd do this?" He dropped his head and captured the incensed words before they left her mouth.

She tasted divine. Anger, mixed with lust, mixed with Maggie's unique scent of...he couldn't put a finger on it. It'd been driving him crazy since he met her. She had a familiar floral scent, but with a touch of sweetness that drove him absolutely nuts.

Deepening the kiss, his tongue delved inside. And was greeted by sharp teeth.

"Ow!" He reared back, letting her hands go, and rolling to the side. He tasted blood, but he'd already healed.

She sat up, anger radiating from her, her eyes slightly glowing. "I am an adult shifter female, but it doesn't mean I need to give in to my baser desires—mate or not."

The nipples poking through her shirt revealed she needed something. She noticed the direction of his gaze and crossed her arms.

Seducing his mate *should not* be this difficult. "I don't get it, Maggie. Casual sex is part of our DNA. Surely, you've been out experimenting."

"I've done my share." The mulish pout to her lips belayed her experience. She thought he might condemn her, but why would he? Sex was natural.

"Forget the fact that we're mates if that bothers you." *And why does it again?* "How is this different from picking a dude up at a club and hitting it wherever it's convenient?"

Her mouth worked. She wanted to tell him to fuck off, he could feel it, but there was something else there. Something she was—he inhaled deeply to determine the emotion—embarrassed about confessing.

Raised human.

His eyes flew wide. "Holy shit, you haven't been with a shifter?" The swell rose from his belly until his laughter boomed through the room.

Oomph. Maggie punched him in the stomach, but it didn't faze him.

When he died down to normal breathing, he grinned wide enough to show his incisors. "Oh beautiful, you are in for a treat."

Ahhh, there it was. The desire he'd scented from her all night hit an all-time high. She drew the corner of her lower lip in, chewing on it because she couldn't take her eyes off his hint of fang.

The idea of being Maggie's first shifter lay was a damn fine feeling. His chest might have puffed up—just a little.

"I'm not having sex with you tonight when we're on the run, I'm afraid for my mother, and you claim we're mates. I haven't needed to see my previous bedmates again, but you'll still be here."

"You bet your sweet ass." Porter laid back, lacing his fingers behind his head. She tensed to get off the bed. "Why not have just a taste, Mage. Relieve your pressure."

She blinked and frowned, but she didn't correct him. It was her name, he'd make her get used to it. Just like she needed to accept that Lobo Springs was her home. Her life had changed in a day and she'd been taking it in stride, but from the emotions drifting through her features, she wasn't as unaffected as she appeared. Not by the news of Lobo Springs, the attack, or especially him.

He internally rejoiced when her decision settled into her gaze. Any relief she took with him would effectively ease his own pressure.

Smoothly, she swung a leg over him, sitting astride his body, and anchored her hands on his shoulders, her hair hanging down to curtain her face. Porter sucked in a breath.

"Did you mean to intimidate me? Or think I couldn't resist you?" She rocked on the erection trapped between them. "I'm not a victim looking for a hero."

"Never thought you were." He unlaced his hands, his fingers aching to touch her skin again.

"Leave them there. I'm in charge."

Deciding the turn of events was more than acceptable, he settled back, hands behind his head. She seemed captivated by the way his biceps flexed, the lick of her gaze running from them to his bare chest, down his washboard stomach.

Betcha never seen this before on your human partners, Porter thought smugly. Shifters were lean and mean, but carpentry kept him in prime condition.

Her pink tongue flicked out, wetting her bottom lip.

His growl vibrated between them. Her eyes flew up to his.

"Are you growling?"

"As a male does when he's incredibly turned on." Her long mane swayed. He had future plans for that hair. It'd be perfect to yank her head to the side while he drove into her from behind, baring her neck for his mark.

She continued to rock over him, her eyes glassy with passion.

"It'd feel better with your jeans out of the way." His voice was as heavy as his balls dying to be released by her touch.

"Not a chance," she panted. The seam of her jeans dug into his sensitive skin. He was never one for pain for pleasure—until now.

"Your sweatshirt," he rasped.

She hitched a breath, her pace unaltered. She whipped it off, throwing it behind her.

Fuuuck. Porter quit breathing, his hands drifting to her bouncing, creamy breasts, contained in a lacy black bra.

"What'd I tell you about your hands?" Grinding down harder, her breaths coming faster, she was getting close.

He snapped his hands back because no way in hell did he want to give her a reason to stop, he enjoyed the show.

She didn't close her eyes, drop her head back, and use him for her pleasure. Riding him without mercy, she explored his body. Hands raked up and down his torso, drifting over his nipples, up his arms—that was his favorite. Her breasts threatened to spill out of their cups, and if he lifted his head an inch, he'd catch one between his teeth.

Getting her off in her pants wasn't what he intended for their first experience. An orgasm was not just another orgasm. She deserved to know what he could do for her. Be fully informed about their mating compatibility.

Until then, he waited, gritting his teeth, fingernails drawing blood to keep his hands off her.

Maggie's eyes glazed, her body melting into the impending climax. Porter flipped her onto her back, snapping her pants clasp and dragging them off her.

"What are you—" She sounded like a pissed female who'd been denied her happy ending, about to attack him, barely noticing he was between her legs, pushing them to the sides.

"Showing you what a real orgasm is," he growled. He could come from the sight. A flushed, furious Maggie, legs spread, her wet, pink center throbbing for him.

He descended. The first swipe of his tongue, Maggie collapsed back with a cry. The second swipe, she raised her knees higher, threading her hands into his hair.

"Porter!" She pressed him closer, undulating her hips.

The third swipe, she jacked her hips up. She was so wet, he made it his goal to lick her up, everything she had. As he tongued her again, he inserted a finger.

"Oh my—" Curled around his face, her entire concentration rested on his tongue and finger like she depended on them to finish her pleasure. "More."

A second finger slid inside her sweltering sex. She convulsed around him, her first orgasm kicking off. He'd find out how many she could tolerate. And increase it from there.

She shook and cried, he raised his eyes to her chest. Across the expanse of her flat belly was her jiggling breasts, defying odds still bound by the weak bra.

Porter ground his erection into the sheets, desperately seeking release when all he wanted to do was bury himself to the hilt and feel his balls smack against her ass.

Her walls eased around his fingers. Dipping his chin down, he firmed his tongue and speared her.

"Porter," she gasped, "I can't."

He withdrew only to say, "I'll show how much you can," and went back to tasting her, rolling his tongue, flicking it to feel her body jump. He returned to her swollen clit, his fingers setting a lazy thrusting rhythm.

Maggie sagged into the mattress, her grip leaving his hair to twist the sheets.

God, she was amazing. Her sweet taste provoked his wild side. How he wasn't frantically humping her he didn't know, but he wouldn't. He'd pushed her farther than she'd planned—ever. Tonight was about her pleasure and what he could do for her.

But he needed something. It wasn't easy palming himself, but propped on one elbow and his knees, he jerked himself off, timing her release with his.

"Yes! Yes! Yes!" Maggie came a second time.

He wasn't done.

"Porter," Maggie pushed at his head, "seriously, I can't."

He raised his head enough to stab her with a dominating stare. "You can. Your body was made to orgasm for me—over and over again."

Her eyes widened at the reminder that they were destined. To distract her, he sucked on her clit and quirked his fingers inside.

Instant orgasm.

Like the starved male he was, he lapped her up. Every time she released, it was his. When the pressure almost drove him to claim her the way they were meant to, he used his hand on himself.

He didn't know how long they were at it. Her voice was hoarse, he was having the time of his life, but the pounding on the door stalled them both.

A growl escaped Porter, but Maggie's startled "down boy" silenced him.

"Uh…" a nervous voice called from the hallway, "I've been getting some noise complaints…"

"We're done." Maggie slid back and tried to sit up, but flopped back down. Her breasts jiggled with movement.

"Next time," he crawled up her body, slick with her desire, and sucked in a nipple through the material, releasing it to say, "I'm going to give these the attention they deserve."

She slid her legs together like they weighed a metric ton each. "You're so confident there's going to be a next time."

Gazing down at her, his erection heavy between them, he glanced between it and her until she looked at his shaft.

"Don't tell me you aren't a little curious how earth shattering it'd be between us."

Mesmerized, she didn't take her eyes off it. He knew he was well-endowed among his kind. Among humans…the answer read clearly in her face. Like comparing a brick to a cinder block. A two-by-four to a railroad tie.

"It would be just like between me and other shifters." Maybe she was going for boasting, but the quiver in her voice negated it. "I don't have a shifter partner comparison."

"I'd be better than your human sex," he admitted, "but there's a reason shifters remain mated for years, and it's not because females like to fake orgasms for centuries."

"Centuries?" she echoed.

With a sigh, he rolled to the side, dragging her into him. Surprisingly, she didn't resist. A bonus to his cunnilingus.

"I'm not kidding, Maggie. We're made for each other. Give us a chance."

"I want to make sure my mom is safe first." She settled into his arms. "Then we'll talk about this mating business and what it means," she murmured, before falling into a deep sleep.

Porter's crazed hard-on didn't let him drift off so quickly; he had to wait until the throbbing subsided. She wanted her mom safe first. Fair enough. Lobo Springs was his first priority, until he found his mate. Now settling her fears took precedence, but his home was a close second.

So be it. They'd find Armana after he got some sleep.

Chapter Six

Maggie woke to muted sunlight streaming through the threadbare curtains. No blankets clung to her body, but she was *hot*. The delicious sensation of a hard body pressed against her back with a steel band wrapped around her waist threatened to lull her back to sleep.

With a deep inhale to help wake herself completely, her senses flooded with the masculine smell of freshly sawed lumber.

Her eyes flew open.

Holy smokes, she was in bed with Porter! Mortification wiped away the cozy feeling of security. Sweet Mother Earth, he'd played with her body, stringing out more orgasms than she'd had in the last year. Absolutely she knew shifters liked sex and a lot of it. Her mother hadn't smothered her entirely. Maggie had gotten "the talk" and for weeks afterward died of embarrassment around her mother.

What Armana failed to educate Maggie on was how sexual they were and how drastically different shifter males were from human men. Everything from anatomy to the ability to wring out orgasms in the double digits—*without penetration.* Night and day.

To think she almost scoffed at Porter when he said he was going to show her a real orgasm. Her original thought had been *puh-lease.* In the years she'd been sexually active, she'd developed her routine for picking up bed partners. Her choices weren't the boastful guys who trolled for women to prove the virtues of sleeping with them. She chose the men with quiet confidence who genuinely cared about what a girl wanted, what she did for a living. It translated to dedication to mutual pleasure in the bedroom. They didn't need the biggest package or the best body, all they needed was laser focus on what made the girl's body sing.

Porter was more than well-endowed, bordered on arrogant in bed, and lacked any doubts that sex with him would be amazing. From what she experienced, he was right—one orgasm was not like another. Then there was his body. She'd nearly choked on lust when she discovered he'd come to bed naked and found herself underneath a wall of solid muscle and virile male.

Very virile.

He'd released himself several times during their tryst and he'd still been long and hard when she succumbed to her exhausted post-coital state.

Most of all, he'd respected her wishes to refrain from full blown sex. He could've impaled her and had his way with her for hours after the first flick of his tongue. Arguing had plummeted far on her priority list.

Just like extracting herself from the cocoon of his body bottomed out on her must-do list.

Mate.

Did that mean she wouldn't feel this intense attraction with other males? Not many other shifters had crossed her path in the past, and they never seemed to realize she was one of them. Their scent was so obvious; hers must be subdued. From the human world?

Asking Porter was an option. So was cringing at his reaction. She would not be ashamed for not knowing about Porter's world. Did he know about the ins and outs of the college financial aid system with the added level of fake documents and an apparently fake name?

Mage Troye.

Porter had called her Mage.

She had liked it.

At the time, he could've called her Sex Bunny Sixty-nine and she would've purred.

"What's going on in that pretty little head of yours?" his baritone rumbled into her ear.

Instantly, it was like none of the orgasms had happened. Her body became primed and ready for him.

He nuzzled the back of her neck, his arm closing tighter around her.

Her first instinct was to wiggle her butt back into the solid line of cock pressing into it.

Suppressing it was—pathetically—very difficult. Instead, she rolled out, his arm going lax to let her escape.

The only clothing that survived the night was her bra, which showed as much as it covered. Her pants and sweatshirt lay strewn around the room.

Porter's gaze heated, his demeanor predatory. She wanted to be his prey. His body was on full display and she couldn't rip her gaze away from him.

Look away. Look away. LOOK AWAY.

"We need to find Ma." Her breathless voice conflicted with her words.

"What's really going on, Mage?" Proving he was yet again stronger than her, his eyes stared solidly into hers. The raging erection and tensed muscles her only indication he yearned to drag her back under him.

"You need to get dressed."

"Nudity doesn't bother shifters," he said archly.

An image of a village of nude males as stunning as Porter, and females just as gorgeous, hit Maggie. "Do shifters wander around naked all day?" The idea of Porter surrounded by buck naked females caused Maggie's fangs to throb, yearning to rip imagined females' throats out.

Porter chuckled, the low sound rumbling between them. "It's not unusual to pass someone on our runs, whether we're heading out or coming back."

Whatever that meant. She heard, *we walk around naked and enjoy it*, and she wasn't going to ask if it was accurate.

"I need your phone to call Ma again." Her eyes widened. "They can't track us through the phones can they?"

"The colony doesn't have the technology. Even with what Seamus has pirated from humans, I doubt he can afford it."

"Sounds like a real nice guy."

Porter's expression turned serious. "He's why we need you."

Not that again. Maggie didn't know what she'd have to do to dissuade him from continuing down the you're-Lobo-Springs-savior path. Becoming head of a town, pack, or whatever Porter called it, caused her to feel just as restless as punching in for a shift at the daycare.

"My mother first."

Porter considered her for a moment. "You can use the bathroom first."

Relieved she started for the bathroom, then recalled her clothing situation. Locating her sweatshirt, she grabbed it off the floor and found her pants—inside out—lying nearby. Porter tracked her the entire time. She managed to bend over without flashing him a close-up of a full moon. From the spike of lust in the room, she figured he wouldn't have minded, probably hoped for it.

Scurrying into the bathroom, she was closing the door when she noticed his pants and shirt hanging up. She tossed them outside the door. "You can dress while I'm in here." Please. Teasing her with his body was cruel and unusual.

Maggie jumped in the shower, scrubbing off quickly. The loss of Porter's scent covering her skin registered as undesirable. She felt stripped without his scent enveloping her.

Mates.

Like, *the rest of her life* mate.

Using the blow dryer was a delay tactic. She could fan her hair and dry it faster than the ancient piece of crap dryer, but then she'd have to leave the bathroom. It's not like she could linger, styling her hair and putting on makeup. She was lucky there was the square inch soap bar.

Finger combing through the long, damp strands, she rescued the hair tie and secured her mane back in a haphazard bun.

Once dressed, she faced the door, took a deep breath, and firmly told her body not to go crazy around the male.

She pulled the door open and determined it was useless. Porter's scent surrounded her once again and her body reacted.

Ugh. Was she in heat, or it was it always like this around shifter males?

Porter sat on the edge of the disheveled bed. The bedspread rested half on, half off the bed, the sheets twisted. Her cheeks burned seeing the evidence while Porter casually flipped through an old yellow pages.

He glanced back at her. "It's all right, Mage. There's nothing to be embarrassed about."

That was the benefit to dating humans. She could lie through her sharp teeth and they were clueless.

"I suppose you do this all the time?" No, that *wasn't* jealousy, just defensiveness.

"Not as much as you'd think. Some males do, but once Seamus took over..." Porter slammed the book down. "I didn't want his castaways, couldn't trust 'em. My pack is like family so that rules them out. When the urge struck, I came here to Freemont."

He stood, stalking toward her. The plaid button up hung in his hand, his snug t-shirt tantalizing her because now she knew what was underneath. The jeans hung on his lean waist and knowing he went commando would've dampened her panties—if she wore any.

Handing her the phone, he towered over her. "What about you Mage?" He cocked his head, a teasing tilt to his lips. "Did you have to find more than one bedmate for the night to satisfy you, or did you go home and finish for yourself what the human boys couldn't?"

Oh no he didn't...didn't guess that's exactly what she'd done. Her experiences had been pleasurable enough, they just weren't *enough*.

"Yeah," he drawled, "thought so. You don't have to worry about that anymore."

Snatching the phone, she ignored him, and dialed her mom.

Both of them turned somber as it rang and rang.

"Shit," Maggie said, on the verge of tears.

"Hey." Porter caressed her face with the back of his hand. "She's been through worse than this. She's a fighter and survivor. We'll find her."

Shakily, Maggie nodded, turning into his hand.

Gently, he took the phone from her and pocketed it. "We'll grab something to eat first. Down the street there's a used car shop. I'll buy a cheap beater to take us to the Guardians."

"What if she's—"

"She's not." He rested his hands on her shoulders until she looked up at him. "You didn't know about mates, so you don't know what's it's like to lose one, right? It's the worst thing that can happen to a shifter. Very few survive the death of a mate, and those who do have children to keep them going. Armana survived the attack, her mate and a son getting killed, and raised two kids alone in basically a whole new world. She's tougher than you think."

"She's all I have."

"Not anymore. You have me and your brother now, too."

If he had just said Jace, she'd still be uneasy, but comforted. Adding himself complicated her situation further. Tall, dark, and sexy stormed into her life when it had been completely unsettled, and as much as he claimed it should reassure her, it didn't. Her emotional state requested handling one situation at a time.

"There's a fast food place a couple blocks from here. We'll function better on a full stomach." He grabbed her hand; she ambled along behind him.

Hunger gnawed at her. Shifter appetites required meat and more meat. She hadn't eaten since the meal with her mom and her purse was probably getting pawed through—pun intended—by Seamus' lackeys, who probably had killer headaches, hell bent on revenge.

Porter planned to feed two shifters on the run and buy a POS. She examined his back pocket. Gawd, the male had an ass. Forcing herself to stay on the wallet outline, she noticed it wasn't terribly thick. No wad of cash, but maybe he had electronic funds?

The closer they got to food, the stronger the smells became. Her stomach rumbled. Porter threw an amused glance over his shoulder. She glared back, on the verge of hangry. He couldn't have eaten any more than she had, but he didn't seem to suffer.

Entering the eatery, she had two orders mentally tallied. One option that would get her by, and one just in case Porter had a credit card with no limit.

He inclined his head toward the cashier who looked barely old enough to be out of elementary school. "Go ahead."

"Can I order what I want?"

The pubescent cashier raised an eyebrow at Porter.

"Knock yourself out," Porter answered.

"Are you serving lunch yet?" The boy nodded. "Four double cheeseburgers, two large fries, and…oh, and the monster burger with the bacon. And a chocolate milkshake."

Usually Maggie took her order to-go and said things like "they want" and "she said to get her this" to pretend it all wasn't for her. Today, the cashier's eyes remained wide as he waited for Porter's order.

"The same," he said.

The cashier paused like he was waiting for Porter to say he was joking before he punched it in. "Uh…is it for here?"

"Sure is." Porter handed a few twenties to the kid. They stood back to wait for their food. "I think you impressed him."

Maggie smirked. "I don't know if impressed is the right word." She glanced around them. Booths were half-filled with people minding their own business. Her gaze lingered on the gigantic windows lining the walls. "Is it safe to eat here?"

"As safe as any. The three shifters who came after you likely drove around all night. If they found us, we'd have been attacked by now. I'll use my credit card to buy the car. Seamus' moles in the bank will notify him, but we'll be across the river in West Creek, on our way to your brother."

A tray with a heap of food waited for them. Porter grabbed it and followed Maggie to a booth. They ate in silence. Maggie's mind wandered to her mother.

"We'll find her," Porter said around a mouthful of fries.

She would've scowled, but she was filling her face with greasy meat. She had practiced hiding her emotions around her mom, but Porter picked up on them instantly. Either her mom's senses had dulled, or she'd been humoring Maggie and shifter's senses were more superb than Maggie realized.

Of course she knew hers were far superior to a human's, she just hadn't understood how she couldn't be sensed by other shifters. Her lack of knowledge of his world put her at a serious disadvantage.

"What's wrong?"

He did it again! She could brush it off, or she could just ask. He had enough proof of how sheltered she'd been. "How do you do that? Sense me so easily? Is it just me or is this normal?"

He stopped chewing and sat back, wiping his fingers off on a napkin. "You are easier to read, but it could be because of our connection."

"We've know each other less than twenty-fours." Sure, they'd connected well enough during the night, but for her to be *special*?

"We're mates."

He said it so simply. They were hot for each other—boom. Eternity together.

She could really use a long talk with her mother.

"We'd better get going." He cleaned up the mess and dumped the tray while she wrapped up the remains of her last burger to eat on the way. "Time to buy a car."

***

Porter considered his options. A single cab pick-up with pockets of rust all over the body for a grand. Or for five hundred more, a late model sedan that'd seen better days sat tucked into the corner of the lot.

Porter faced the salesman. "How's the truck run?" Porter inhaled slow and purposeful. The sickly aroma of a lie forming teased his nostrils. He waited for the salesman lay it on heavy.

Maggie coughed into her hand. "I'd say it runs as badly as it looks."

The salesman visibly switched tactics. "It's all superficial. There's nothing wrong with how it runs."

Maggie made a sound of derision. "So the previous owners paid meticulous attention to the engine, but let the body rot? How about the other relic you pointed out?"

The odor emanating from the man changed. He wouldn't have to lie so heartily. "The car's really a bargain. No one's wants a vehicle that's more boxy than sleek, so we're just interested in getting it off the lot."

Maggie crossed her arms and eyed it dubiously. "How's it run?"

Porter repressed a smile. Maggie's voice held an edge; she meant business. He shut his mouth, clasped his hands behind him, and let Maggie do the talking.

"It purrs like a kitten." The salesman answered with confidence. His smell said otherwise.

She chuckled. "A thirty-year-old car doesn't purr, it roars. I can see the holes in the muffler from here. All I'm asking is will it break down after a few miles, or will it run for a few hundred before it needs money poured into it?"

The man's eyebrows shot up. "It...It'll run for miles. Might blow smoke, but she runs good enough."

"We'll take it for eight."

It was the salesman's turn to cough. "We're already selling it at a bargain."

"Nope. Bet you couldn't give it away." Maggie tapped her foot in a show of impatience. Porter sensed no urgency from her. She'd barter all day. "Eight-fifty."

"Perhaps if you were willing to consider thirteen-hundred, we could talk."

"Nine and we're running out of time. There's plenty of used lots in Freemont."

"Twelve hundred," the salesman shot back.

Maggie adopted a regretful look. "I'm not going higher than a grand because that's all we have. Gas for that thing will cost how much?"

The human glanced between Maggie and the old car, blew out a breath, his eyes skipping back and forth. "Deal."

Porter drew out his card. The paperwork was minimal and he lied on most of it.

The keys were handed over and he and Maggie were on their way.

"How'd you learn to do that?"

Maggie paused in her search of all the compartments in the mothball-smelling ride. "What, barter?"

"Yeah, you were ruthless."

"Not really. If I were, I'd have taken it for five, but we were in a hurry." She settled back into the sofa-like seat. "Ma was the ruthless one. If she could sniff out a deal, she went for it." Maggie lifted a shoulder. "We didn't have much money. I remember her driving us around in a car a lot like this one."

Explains how she knew its gas consumption was absurd.

"Next time I need to make a big purchase," Porter leaned toward her to whisper, "I'm bringing your mother."

Just when he'd been thinking he could function decently around her intoxicating beauty without his body going haywire, she laughed. It wasn't her beauty or strength affecting him this time, but her personality. And he liked it.

Her whole life had been turned upside down. She survived a kidnapping attempt and feared for her mother, yet she was ready to tackle the world next.

She was exactly what he needed to overthrow Seamus.

They crossed into West Creek. Buildings got older, the area poorer. Nearly all the way through, on the outskirts of town, he pointed out Pale Moonlight, a proud building standing among rundown industrial businesses.

"Jace used to work there?" Her nose pressed to the window, he didn't miss the longing in her voice.

Through an ugly situation, at least he could reunite her with her brother.

Porter continued out of town. He'd never made it to the Guardian's headquarters when he'd been looking for Jace, but he knew the general area. If the Guardians sensed a couple of shifters in trouble near their property, they'd find them. If

Armana had made it already, then they'd be expecting them and lift their wards.

Maggie scanned around them, intent on their surroundings. "I've never been outside of city limits."

"Seriously?" Porter couldn't imagine living *within* city limits. Shifters craved fresh air, needed to run regularly—on four legs.

He flicked his gaze to the review mirror— and left it there. The morning had been going so smoothly; he'd actually enjoyed himself, but the good spirit drained out of him.

Maggie sensed the change in him and turned around. "Oh shit. The van."

"They knew we'd try to find the Guardians and camped by the road out of town." Porter pressed down on the gas pedal.

The speedometer climbed higher. Every bump a smooth up and down motion as the old car glided over the road.

"They're getting closer." Maggie's hands clutched the head rest, her body twisted in the seat.

"We'll never out run them, and I don't know the exact directions. Hold on." He hit the brakes, yanked the wheel to the right, and slammed on the gas again. The big boat of a car fishtailed onto a gravel road.

Maggie bounced across the seat into him. She scrambled back to her post, watching out the rear window.

Porter quickly gained control, the car maneuvering over gravel with ease. He spotted another turn; took the left as fast as he dared. Maggie thumped against the passenger door, quickly righting herself.

The road was poorly maintained, shrubbery intruding from each side.

Perfect. He slowed and eased off the road, parking as deep into the trees as the car could fit.

Maggie glanced around her in alarm. "What are you doing?"

"Stopping before they can follow our dust cloud. We run from here, get a head start." He jumped out, motioning for Maggie to do the same.

Maggie wrestled out against all the limbs pressing in on the door. "Run through the woods? What if they catch us?"

"I've seen them run their wolves. They're big, but slow as hell." Porter stripped off his shirt and made quick work of his shoes and pants.

Maggie watched him with eyes as big as saucers. "You mean…you want to shift and run?"

"What else would I mean? Have them chase us through the trees as humans?" He laughed at the absurd thought.

Maggie gulped, her gaze dropping away.

I was raised as a human.

Oh. Shit. "Please tell me you've shifted before."

She didn't reply. Her stance answered for her.

A shifter who'd never shifted. How the hell was he supposed to train her, an adult? He didn't know a shifter who'd gone through puberty without experiencing the transition.

They stood no chance on foot against the three pursuing them.

"Strip down," he ordered.

Her hands fisted the bottom of her shirt; she hesitated.

"Maggie," he barked, startling her. "If you want to make it to safety, you need to move."

She ripped off her sweatshirt and climbed out of her pants. Standing naked and gorgeous, he wished he had time to leisurely marvel over her curves. He heard a motor in the distance.

"Close your eyes, take a few calming breaths." Her lids drifted closed and he described what he normally felt when he transitioned. "Listen to that voice. You've heard it your whole life. It's our intuition, our instinct, the force behind our senses. Tune into that voice, that feeling."

Fear and unease faded; a sense of wonder emanated from her. He remembered feeling the same during his first shift all those years ago.

"Let it take over. Your body knows what to do, even if your conscious mind doesn't."

Hurry up, hurry up. The distant engine was getting closer. Their pursuers hadn't found the road they'd hidden on yet.

Maggie's eyes flew open. "I can't." She clenched her hands at her sides. "I don't know how."

"Breathe, Maggie. Relax. You're scared and it's smothering your wolf. Let her take care of you."

"There is no wolf inside of me." Anguish overtook her expression, and if she let it rule her, she'd never shift.

"It's not like a separate being within us." He scanned around them, at their clothes strewn around. "Think of it as clothing. We're born naked, but we can get dressed. The clothes are like a part of us when we're wearing them. But they don't take over our body."

It was a shit analogy, but he had no other way to explain it.

Maggie nervously licked her lips and nodded. "Okay. I'm going to put on my wolf costume."

Wheels crunching to a stop drifted through the trees. They found the road.

Porter controlled his breathing, kept lying to himself, saying they had plenty of time so Maggie's concentration wouldn't be affected by his apprehension.

Her form began to change. She gasped and lost the shift. Her eyes squeezed shut. A large, black wolf with light blue eyes stood in her place. She whimpered and barked, looking perplexed.

"Telepathy," he said before he shifted.

Maggie pranced back from his wolf, surprised to suddenly have a large muddy brown wolf towering over her.

Porter switched to mind-speak.

Communicate like this.

Sharp blue eyes narrowed on him. Okay? Then her wolf appeared extremely happy.

He couldn't help his tongue lolling out at her delight. *Follow me. We need to move quickly and quietly. Mind-speak if you have trouble keeping up.*

Her shaggy black head dropped in a nod.

Porter took off.

They swiftly ran through trees, ducking under low hanging branches. Porter pushed the pace, waiting for the signal from Maggie to slow down.

She remained on his tail. Literally.

Howls behind him spurred even faster.

Only two wolves chased them. Did one of them stay behind with the vehicles?

He had no idea where they were going. Guardians were known for the wards surrounding their land, keeping them camouflaged, disorienting unwanted visitors.

Since Seamus' thugs knew where they were and would try to herd them away, Porter changed tactics.

He slowed long enough to howl. Maggie rang out behind him, her voice clear and beguiling, like the creature herself.

They raced through the woods. There was no indication before he slammed into an invisible ward. With a sharp yelp, he was flung backward, tumbling through the brush, crashing to a stop against a tree trunk.

Porter! Maggie skidded to a stop in time to only bump against the force.

He tried to rise, shaking his head. His eyes blinked against the pain. It took two attempts before he was back on all fours.

Their pursuers closed in.

Open up! Maggie yelled mentally.

Porter fervently hoped others could hear her. They had to be sitting outside of Guardian property to have encountered their protections.

Maggie simultaneously howled and yelled mental commands to let them in. Porter swayed on his feet, pain in his ribs making breathing excruciating. His head pounded and he was lucky he didn't break his neck. It would've taken hours to heal from such an injury.

Porter sensed Brutus and his injuries became inconsequential as a shadow launched through the air toward Maggie. He leapt, knocking Brutus off course. They rolled, tangled together, snapping and biting. Teeth ripped into Porter's hide, fire raced up his side as claws tore at his flank. His brain barely registered the pain. Protecting his mate overrode any other sensation besides the rage he used to keep Brutus down. Jaws clamped down on a wedge of muscle, Porter raised his eyes, his adrenaline heightened senses picking up another shifter.

The second attacker, Cletus, stalked Maggie who was snarling, her fangs bared. Porter fought Brutus with everything he had, determined to get to Maggie. She was strong, but fighting the other wolf during her first shift wouldn't end well.

Porter was covered in burning claw marks and bites. Brutus wore just as many. His muzzle bloodied and raw, he snapped at any part of Brutus he could sink his fangs into. He managed to wrestle the other wolf under him with his jaws at the male's neck, breaking through skin, filling his taste buds with the male's sickening flavor. Whines escaped Brutus; Porter was relentless. He increased the pressure, shaking his head to do as much damage as possible.

The second male growled, his patience with Maggie's standoff growing thin. His haunches tensed, ready to spring. Porter dropped Brutus, using his hide for traction as he pivoted to attack the male before he got to Maggie.

A large form flew through the air from behind Maggie. The giant black wolf dived onto the wolf about to attack Maggie. Maggie danced back, her eyes reflecting the shock Porter felt.

Leaves crunched behind him, Porter spun, prepared for attack. Brutus bunched to lunge up, teeth bared, neck dripping blood. A shot rang out. The ground sprayed out next to Brutus.

"I wouldn't move," a female voice called out.

Both he and Porter froze.

Porter couldn't scent her, concealed behind the wards, but he had determined the identity of the wolf engaged with Maggie's attacker.

Movement behind the wall of protection dragged his attention off the big wolf who fought Maggie's attacker, Cletus.

Two imposing males held their guns aimed at him and Brutus.

A blond with dark blue eyes waved his gun. "Shift."

Porter flowed onto two legs. "Maggie!" She hovered too close to the grappling males, enthralled. "Maggie, back away."

Her eyes flicked to him, then back to the fighters. She whined and moved her feet, like she wanted to jump in and help the giant black wolf. But there was no need. He pinned Maggie's attacker.

Next to him, Brutus flowed into his human form. "Guardians, our leader has commanded this male be brought in."

"For what?" Porter snapped.

"Shut it." The demand came from the male with silver gleaming through his dark hair and eyes.

Porter followed commands, hoping his acquiescence supported his innocence of whatever crazy tale Brutus came prepared with.

Brutus' companion pawed the ground in submission, the wolf backed off him. Both males shifted. Cletus lay bleeding in the leaves, and a tall male with a shaved head and ice blue eyes stood over him.

Porter switched his attention to Maggie, who was spellbound. It was the first time she'd seen Jace in well over ten years. She must've recognized his scent, knew the wolf was her estranged brother. She couldn't tear her gaze away from his.

"Maggie," Jace said softly. "It's okay. You can shift back."

The wolf's eyes swept across the four nude males surrounding her.

"Can I talk to her?" Porter asked the males with their guns trained on the group. He looked toward Jace. "This is all new to her."

Jace's brows drew down and it dawned on him that Maggie had remained sheltered all this time. He glanced at Maggie then back at Porter who nodded and mouthed *first time shifting*. Jace's eyes widened, incredulous.

Everyone's naked! Maggie's scream tore through Porter's mind. He recoiled, the other males shook their heads, still ringing from her mental shout. Her words had reached the entire group.

"Can she borrow one of your shirts?" Porter requested, grateful the two males with guns were still clothed.

They shot him a *say whaaat?* look.

"What the fuck for?" The blond's tone said Porter's request was ridiculous.

"Bennett, please." Jace yanked Cletus to his feet and shoved the bleeding male forward. "Don't fuck around, wolf. A damn good sniper's got you in her crosshairs."

"This is *Maggie* Maggie?" Bennett eyed her dubiously.

Both Jace and Porter nodded.

Bennett scowled, but he untucked his shirt to pull off while Mercury waved Brutus and Porter to start walking.

Porter didn't move. "I'm with her."

Mercury's expression turned droll. "What about this situation makes you think you can call the shots?"

"I'm her mate."

Jace's head whipped up, glaring at him, assessing him. Porter withstood his scrutiny.

"Maggie?" Jace wanted her confirmation.

Porter tensed wondering what she'd say.

The wolf managed to lift one shoulder in the canine version of a shrug.

"That idea's new to her, too." Porter explained.

Bennett tossed his tech shirt to Jace. The wards must be down to allow them through.

"This is how it's gonna go. You two brutes take the lead." Bennett gestured to Brutus and Cletus. "You," he waved to Porter, "walk behind. Jace and Maggie bring up the rear. One suspicious move and I'll tranq your ass and drag your bare bottom through the woods so you can get dirt in all the right places." His navy blue eyes were full of promise. "Uh, except you, Maggie."

"Move it," Mercury ordered. "Don't forget Kaitlyn likes to test her range."

Porter moved into place, looking over his shoulder. Jace held the shirt out toward her, facing away. Maggie was intelligent enough to figure out shifting in reverse was the same. She flowed into her statuesque form, snatched the shirt, and pulled it on. Porter didn't like another male's scent on her skin, but he smelled female all over Bennett's shirt. The strength of the scent suggested he and the female were mated. Mercury smelled the same, only his mate's scent indicated a human woman.

Two mated males and her brother. Porter couldn't have asked for better Guardians to protect her.

Chapter Seven

Holy shit.
Holy shit.
For real?

Maggie shuffled along, holding down the hem of the shirt the blond gave her. He was a big male, and if she was a normal sized human, she'd swim in it. But she was a solid shifter female and the bottom of the shirt rested just below her ass cheeks. None of the males gave her a second look even when every inch of skin had been bare. The two brutes hadn't leered at her, their primary goal to persuade the Guardians they were carrying out Seamus' perfectly valid orders.

She concentrated on navigating through the trees. Wherever they were going, there'd better be clothing. She needed a few years to get used to the clothing optional way of shifters.

Porter walked in front of her, Jace next to her.

Her brother. Next to her. Tears pricked her eyes. Porter stiffened and Jace glanced at her.

"You, uh, look different." Yet, he didn't.

He was just as tall, more muscle had been packed on, and his thick wavy hair had been shaved. Eyes even lighter than hers stared back at her. The combination made him appear more sinister than he ever had before.

Taken aback, he ran a hand over his stubble. His expression darkened. "Well, get used to it. I was shorn with a silver blade in prison." Meaning it'd never grow back thanks to the silver, and being abruptly reminded about it when she'd been the reason behind it brought out his defensive side.

Maggie inhaled sharply, the reminder of all he'd been through for her slammed back. "I'm so sorry."

How inane it sounded. Like three little words made up for her abandonment.

He shrugged. "That man who kidnapped you deserved to die. I had to pay the price."

"Jace—"

"Not here." He angled his head toward Porter and the two hulks she still didn't know by name. Where could the third shifter be, the one from the van? "We'll talk at the lodge."

Maggie fell silent. The lodge Jace mentioned appeared like a magical illusion puzzle, the ones she'd have to stare at to make out the picture.

It was a giant log cabin. Much like the ski resorts she saw on TV for the rich and famous. But it should have a sign that read *No trees were harmed in the making*. Except for the building material, of course. The lodge was situated within the trees like it'd grown up among them. The rugged road that circled to the front door was like an accessory to the unique beauty of the building. Large pane windows reflected nature back to the viewer making it seem as if it was part of the woods.

She studied their surroundings. Cabins were tucked deep into the trees, hardly visible in the foliage. Did these males live in those?

For a girl who'd been raised in the city, it seemed like an alien concept to live so completely in nature. The feeling of rightness couldn't be ignored, her shifter side sighing in satisfaction at the idea.

Her shifter side.

She'd shifted. Into her wolf.

Oh god, it felt like such a bigger deal than losing her virginity to the fumbling college boy who thought he was more experienced than he was.

The change had been wild—pun totally intended.

She'd never felt more alive, all four limbs stretching and bunching with each stride. The race had been exhilarating and it had nothing to do with the males chasing her.

Okay, maybe a little, but she didn't think the intense craving to run would be leaving any time soon.

Maggie trained her eyes to the ground. If she looked up, she'd see Porter's firm ass cheeks, and she didn't need to spike the air with arousal around a bunch of strangers.

Then there was her naked brother next to her. Awkward.

The two burly males ahead of Porter sickened her and not because they were covered in dried blood. Their resolution to take her back to their boss was palpable. A smug cloud hung over them, like they had an ace up their figurative sleeve.

The two dressed males with guns eased her fears a bit, ironically. Like Jace, they oozed confidence and resolve to get to the bottom of her story and what was going on. She smelled a significant female on each one and wondered if that's why she didn't feel an intense attraction to them like she did to Porter. They were stunning male specimens, and she was learning shifter sexual appetites were powerful and instinctual, but her libido said "meh." Her sex drive wanted nothing to do with Hulk One and Two, but they'd tried to kidnap her. It would've been beyond disturbing if she had felt anything hot around them other than her temper.

The other female hidden in the trees, the sniper, piqued her interest. She'd never officially met another female shifter. She'd never officially met another shifter period, other than Jace and her mom, and now she was surrounded by them, in their territory.

Ma! Maggie gasped and tugged on Jace's arm. "Did Ma make it here?" Jace appeared baffled.

She released Jace's arm to surge forward, intent on her two attackers, prepared to draw blood for answers. They tensed, as if daring her to assault them, but she was restrained by her brother and blocked by Porter. "What did you do with her you bastards?" she shouted.

"Wait, Maggie. Why would Ma come *here*?"

"Because these assholes attacked me last night to try to take me back to Lobo Springs. I called her, worried for her safety. She said she'd find you."

A myriad of emotions passed through Jace's features. Maggie's heart wrenched with each one— puzzlement, anger, hope, alarm.

"I know not where your mother's at." Hulk One threw back to them.

"And you're a lying sack of shit, Brutus," Porter snarled.

"Enough!" The one called Bennett monitored Jace's reaction carefully, in case he charged the captors. "We'll get all of your stories in a minute."

They entered the lodge. Jace tossed her a pair of sweats from a stack sitting on a cabinet by the door. He grabbed two more pairs. Bennett picked up a couple more, and Mercury led her two attackers down a hall to the right.

Bennett gave Jace a hard look. "You good?"

"Yeah, man. I'll talk to these two."

A tall, willowy redhead rushed in. Maggie recognized her scent as the sniper.

"Did I miss anything?" she asked, shouldering a long, menacing rifle.

"Just in time, Kaitlyn." Jace tossed Porter a pair of sweats and climbed into his own.

Kaitlyn assessed Maggie, who examined her in return. "This is Cassie's sister-in-law, huh?"

Jace nodded without looking at either one of them. "Maggie. This is Porter, her…"

"Mate," Porter finished.

Jace's jaw ground together. Maggie wondered how badly their first encounter turned out that that much hostility remained.

Kaitlyn ignored the tension. "Interrogation Two or somewhere else?"

Interrogation? Maggie's heart sank. There was no reason for Jace to give her special treatment. He'd saved her from getting mauled, it was more than she deserved from him.

"Yeah, we need to record everything," he answered.

Maggie trudged with them to the interrogation room. Room one was reserved for the thugs. She heard voices rumbling from inside.

The stark room contained a table and four chairs. Porter pulled one out for her. She couldn't help but notice how his sweats slung low on hips, revealing the trail of hair that disappeared under the waistband. She tried to look away, but found herself staring at his chiseled abs. It only got worse from there because the other places to look were his defined pecs and bulging biceps. Carpentry did a body good.

Lifting her gaze farther to keep her out of emotional turmoil, she found his dark eyes lit with humor and a faint smirk on his face. How must she look? She was a frumpy mess with a baggy shirt and sweats too big she had to hold them up. She hoped the shirt hid her braless state. And what about her hair?

Accepting the chair, she settled in, Porter taking the seat next to her. Jace sat across from her, and Kaitlyn leaned against the door, her arms crossed.

Jace spoke first. "The last I heard from this guy is how I needed to save Lobo Springs." Jace pinned Porter with a glare. "I didn't cooperate so you went after her?"

"One of you can save your home without violence and bloodshed." Porter's voice was full of hostility.

"I haven't seen that place since I was *nine*. And my last memory there is the slaughter of my father and brother. It's no home to me."

Maggie's focus stayed on the table top. Their brother. She couldn't remember him. Sometimes in her dreams, she saw a boy with laughing blue eyes twirling her around, and then…darkness. She'd only been four, but it seemed another betrayal, to not remember her dad and brother very well. Like if she'd truly loved them, they should be etched into her memory.

Porter matched Jace's intensity. "It's your birthright."

"Yada, yada, yada." Jace waved him off. The movement drew Maggie's attention to her brother's tattoos, or rather, the scars that lay underneath. They ran down the side of his neck, down his arm and across his chest.

"Jace, what happened?" she breathed.

He turned his vexation toward her. "After all these years, now you want to know?"

"Easy," Porter warned.

She could crawl up in a shell, break down into tears, or...be honest. "Ma was so adamant that you threatened our safety. She cut you off so readily, I was afraid that'd she'd do that to me, too. I had nowhere else to go. Knew no one else. It was selfish, Jace, and I'm sorry. I've thought about you every day. Regretted it every day. I should've tried to find you."

The anger drained from her brother. He slumped back, scrubbed his face, looking exhausted—not physically, but emotionally.

She should know. She felt the same.

"Forget it. It's done. I get it. I know how maniacal Ma was about secrecy and forgetting we were shifters."

"She hasn't changed."

"I believe it." Jace studied her for another moment before switching to Porter. "What happened after we talked?"

"Seamus got worse. Things have really deteriorated in the last few years. The whole colony fears he's turning feral, the clan leaders are becoming as good as powerless. He bribes, blackmails, extorts, whatever it takes. I found the name Mage goes by and sat on it until Seamus came after me and my livelihood."

"And you thought to take my sister back to face a psychopath?"

All eyes were on Porter, who smoldered with ire. "No. I wouldn't let anything happen to her."

"Was that before or after you realized she was your mate?"

Porter sat forward, gaze narrowed on Jace. Kaitlyn inched forward, ready for trouble. "Always," he bit out. "I don't hurt innocents like Seamus does."

Maggie needed to dissolve the aggression in the room or they'd get nowhere. "He found me at work. I told him to hit the road, but he followed me." She wouldn't mention hunting perverts. Not the time. "When I pulled into my apartment complex, I was attacked by Hulk One and Two out there."

Jace blinked. "Who?"

"Brutus and Cletus," Porter answered.

"There were three hulks who came after me," Maggie filled in.

Kaitlyn snickered, covered her mouth to mask a fake cough when all three of them turned toward her.

"Do you know what their intent was? Kill or kidnap?" Jace spoke to both of them. Porter would know the details; Maggie would know from experience.

"Kidnap," Maggie answered. "I heard them say to bring the van around to throw me in."

"It could've been to hide your body." Jace stretched an arm across the empty chair next to him. He eyed Porter. "What's your opinion?"

"Either one would fit Seamus' needs. He's tied up any loose ends that could cost him his leadership position. I was the next one because I'm a vocal supporter of voting." Porter's jaw tightened, his eyes filled with regret. "It's possible someone found out I was searching for you. You're a Guardian and untouchable for Seamus, but Maggie he could use."

"Because I'm a Guardian, I'd think he'd stay far away from her."

"Seamus is ruthless. We knew he was more aggressive, some hoped it was a good sign. No one realized just how aggressive he'd be until it was too late. He didn't have to kill for power, but he did." Porter's nostrils flared. Maggie wondered what memory caused the anguish in the air. "Then it was the rumors he was rough on the females. Clan leaders who spoke against him soon found major trouble in their lives, enough to take their focus off Seamus. Any who thought to overthrow him met with suspicious *accidents*, but by then, everyone was either too afraid of him or under his spell."

Jace considered Porter's story. "But not you?"

"Obviously not under his spell. I knew he always had a mean streak, but I won't let him continue to terrorize."

"Then why didn't you fight for power?" A hint of derision lit Jace's tone.

Maggie shifted, her first instinct was to stand up for Porter. But she wanted to hear the story, too.

A muscle flexed in Porter's jaw, his dark eyes bright with anger. "Do you remember that night?"

Jace's brow creased, knowing exactly which night Porter referred to. "I remember enough," he said gruffly.

"I'm surprised, Jace. You were pretty young."

"I wasn't allowed to fight, and Maggie was only four."

"I was twenty-nine, but the chaos…it messed with all of us. I don't think there was a single family in the colony untouched by the devastation. My mom…my baby sister…" Porter wiped his face like he was trying to scrub the memory away. "My father hung on, using the challenge against Seamus to end himself. I just—I had so many to bury, the pack was looking to me for guidance, I couldn't…" He shrugged helplessly. "I should've. If I challenged him now, my clan would suffer."

Jace's features softened, his faraway stare told Maggie he also went back in time. She had always wished she could remember more, but the anguish from Porter's memory alone…maybe she was the lucky one. Too young to know what she'd lost.

Her brother blew out a heavy breath. "Ma took us away the next night. I had to help with," he glanced at Maggie, "cleanup. We were asleep and she woke us up and that was all for Great Moon. Literally."

Maggie's recollection was vague, dulled. She'd been so young and Jace and her mother had protected her from the worst. "I hardly remember Dad, or Keve."

Uttering his name summoned tears. She hastily wiped them away. It'd been so many years, but occasionally she was reminded of all that had been taken away. Maggie considered her abduction the worst day of her life, but if she'd had any recollection of the village slaughter, it would no doubt make it pale in comparison. How drastically her life must've changed, and she didn't know enough to realize.

Porter rubbed her back, comforting her. Kaitlyn stood silently, not interfering with their moment.

Someone tapped on the door. Maggie hastily wiped her eyes, Jace cleared his throat, and Porter's hand stalled mid-stroke.

"Go ahead," Kaitlyn called.

The door opened to a grim-faced Bennett, an ominous cloud accompanied the shifter. He sat in the chair next to Jace, whose brows were drawn, his shoulders bunched. Maggie's gut churned, she waited for the shoe to drop.

"Denlan," Bennett began, "tell us what happened when you followed Maggie back to her place."

Porter straightened in his seat, his expression guarded. "I parked a block away to wait and see if she went anywhere right away. I planned to talk with her again in the morning. I saw a familiar van, one I've seen Seamus' cronies use. Then I heard the scuffle in the garage. I found a hammer in my toolbox, but it was enough to sneak up on Dugger and knock him out. I jumped Brutus and Maggie knocked out Cletus. We took off."

Relief oozed out of Maggie. She didn't need any more uncomfortable moments and admitting she'd spent the night with Porter would do it.

"You only knocked Dugger out?"

"Yeah," Porter scoffed. "It's more than he deserved. Rumor has it, Maggie's not the only innocent girl he's accosted."

Bennett wore the bad cop interrogating expression she'd seen on detective shows. The innocuous questions before they dropped the bomb. Neither she nor Porter knew what was coming.

"Can anyone else prove that?" Bennett asked.

Porter recoiled, like the question was absurd. "I didn't show off my handiwork. Just grabbed my hammer before we left."

"He was still alive." Maggie's voice hitched because it dawned on her why Bennett was asking.

"Brutus claims that when he and Cletus regained consciousness, Dugger's head had been severed by a saw belonging to you."

Maggie's mouth dropped open; Porter spewed curse words. Jace and Bennett assessed their reaction.

A dude she'd never met was willing to kill his own people to get to her and Porter. It was absurd, shit that only happened on those cop shows she watched. Not in real life. Not to her.

"He also claims Seamus sent them to rescue Maggie from you. That you'd become so obsessed with overthrowing him and taking over that you're willing to go to any lengths to make it happen."

"Bullshit." Porter slammed the table top with his fist. She'd only know him for a day, but knew it was an uncharacteristic outburst for him.

Kaitlyn pushed off the wall; Bennett narrowed his navy blue eyes on Porter; Jace watched her.

~120~

Maggie needed to defend him. She didn't know Seamus, but those brutes had no intention to "help" her. "I sensed no threat from Porter when he came into my work." At the sex shop. A little time to explain that detail would be nice, although considering their reaction to nudity, it may not be a big deal.

"He could've changed tactics once he sensed you were his mate." Jace lifted a brow at Porter. It'd be next to impossible for Porter to prove it.

Porter flattened his hands on the table and leaned over, prompting Kaitlyn to inch closer in case she needed to fling him back. "I *never* planned on hurting Maggie. She's the only way to get rid of Seamus and still survive. The colony *loved* Bane. They'd welcome any of his kin, still hope one of you will come back." He collapsed back, working the issue over mentally. "I carry my main toolbox in the bed of my truck, but I have more in my shop. Since they've been sabotaging my work to drive me out of town, or set me up for a," Porter threw his hands up for air quotes, "'suicide' or 'accident.' I have no doubt they stole one my saws. I'm a carpenter. I have at least five."

His work had been getting messed with? Clearing Porter's name was paramount. The thought of him getting put away into whatever jail shifters used made her want to tear into flesh. "And Porter was with me when I called Mom and now she's missing. He certainly isn't responsible. We've been together the whole time."

~121~

Jace lifted his gaze to Porter. "Unless he had an accomplice."

Maggie worked her mouth, but she couldn't think of anything to say. She had sensed Dugger alive, but if someone came behind them, he was easy pickings. She faced Porter. "Do you know where Ma lives?"

His dark eyes pinned her, wary that she'd turn against him. "Yes."

Still, he didn't smell like he was a lying, murderous bastard and she said so.

"You're right, Maggie," Jace said, "but we have to take Brutus' claims seriously."

Bennett nodded. "And it'll give us access to the colony. Jace, Kaitlyn, you two stay here. I don't need family drama while we're investigating this. Mercury took the other two to a holding cell and he'll remain here in case they cause problems. I'll bring Chayton."

A faint snort of derision from Kaitlyn turned all of their heads. She immediately appeared sweet and innocent, running her hand down the thick red braid swung over her shoulder.

"Who's Chayton?" Maggie asked, attuned to the change in Kaitlyn's demeanor. This Chayton set the red-head's emotions in a speeding car on a winding course.

"He's a seasoned Guardian, but unfamiliar with the area. This'll be a good experience." Bennett shot a hard look toward Kaitlyn, who bobbed her head in compliance.

Were they speaking telepathically? She'd have to ask Porter in private. No reason to highlight how unshifter-like she was—again. Her pride still smarted from earlier.

Maggie asked the next question that came to mind. "What are you going to do with us?"

***

Porter stared at the barred cell with indignation. They wanted to lock him up, away from Maggie, and expected him to just wait.

The tall female, Kaitlyn, had taken Maggie so she could clean up while Kaitlyn scrounged up some clothing for her. Porter hadn't liked the separation, but the droop in Maggie's shoulders prevented him from speaking up. Her worry weighing on her, her reunion with Jace not exactly a happy event, it tore at Porter. He was her male, driven to fix everything for her.

He confronted the surly shifter next to him holding the keys to his cell. "I can help you look for Armana."

"Those weren't Bennett's orders." Jace's tone was a little too smug.

Big brother didn't approve of Porter for Maggie. Big brother could suck it.

"Go tell Maggie that you aren't using every resource to find her mother."

Jace stood inches away, his stance domineering. "She's my mother, too."

"And she's mine now, also." Twirl on that, too, Guardian.

Reproach gleamed in Jace's ice eyes. "Has Maggie accepted you? Has she agreed to the mating ceremony?"

Did she even *know* about the ceremony?

It seemed like for every step ahead Porter took, he was pushed two steps back.

Maggie was his! It was meant to be. He went in search for her to save Lobo Springs, and viola, she was his mate, the cosmic answer to his dilemma. Fate wouldn't have given him Maggie as a mate if she wasn't destined to return with him.

"I don't trust you, Denlan." Jace held open the barred door to the cell. "I don't think you have Maggie's best interest in mind."

Porter stepped inside because fighting the issue would make it worse for him. He didn't forget he was being investigated for murder. "I don't really care what you think. Only Maggie's opinion matters."

"She seems pretty ambiguous toward you." Jace shut the door and stood back.

Porter set his hands on his hips. He wanted to be pissed about Jace's statement, but he was right. Only Porter didn't think it was him per se. She'd even defended him—sort of. "She told me she was raised human. However you grew up, once you left, Armana restricted Maggie even more. She didn't interact with her own kind, she'd never shifted, she knows next to nothing about our world."

With each point Porter made, Jace's expression darkened. "You were serious? Today was her very first time shifting? Ma brought me to the woods for my first transition." His brows drew together as if wondering why she hadn't done the same for Maggie. "She smells human."

"I thought I had the wrong girl when I first scented her. If she didn't look like you," did he just admit the female he lusted over resembled the dude standing in front of him? "and set off my mating instinct, I'd have kept searching."

He thought of mentioning Maggie's hobby of hunting perverts, but it wasn't really his can of beans to spill. If it was imperative for Maggie's safety, he'd share it with Jace. It wasn't and his morbid sense of humor wanted to see how the info got sprung on her asshole brother.

"You should've stayed away from her all together," Jace said.

"Then she would've been taken by Seamus' men."

Jace worked his jaw. "That remains to be seen."

"I didn't kill Dugger, just like my work in Lobo Springs wasn't faulty. I'm being set up." Seamus' skill at making himself appear innocent was obvious to Porter. Would it be just as obvious to the Guardians?

"Sit tight, Denlan." Jace walked away.

Porter fisted his hands, ground his teeth, dragged in ten ragged breaths. If he punched the wall, banged on the door, or displayed his temper, it'd give Seamus more power over how others deemed his character.

Maggie was here. She was safe. Seamus was under investigation just as much as Porter was. He could rest. For now.

***

Maggie lifted the shirts Kaitlyn had flung her direction to land on top of the pile of jeans. The Guardian even had a brand new set of Asics that were only a size larger than she wore. All the clothing still had tags on them.

"Do you like to shop?" Maggie directed her question to the female's ass sticking out of the closet.

Kaitlyn pulled her head out, grinning wolfishly. "A girl can never be too prepared." She sat back on her heels and blew a strand of hair that had slipped out of her braid away from her eyes. "I'm kinda the personal shopper for everyone here. I pick up items for myself, but," she indicated her black cargo pants, long-sleeved black shirt, and heavy black boots, "I don't get out of these nearly as much as I'd like to."

Maggie peered around the cabin for the twentieth time. It was just so cozy. About the size of her apartment, the cabin was tucked deep into the trees. Unlike her apartment, there was a pleasant zone of privacy from others.

The cabin was decked out in eclectic décor and a lot of it. Vintage side tables held modern lamps. Her bedding was a cozy eggplant that blended with the deep floral prints on the walls. None of the artwork matched but still worked together. Kaitlyn's talent for choosing items that complemented each other was apparent throughout the entire, cluttered cabin.

It was so…unwolflike. Maggie didn't know what she'd expected. Their own furnishings had been sparse, but that was due to lack of funds, not her mother's preference. She never considered how her mom would've decorated their place had it been an option. Did shifters prefer pictures of wild animals and nature?

Kaitlyn stood to dig for bras in her dresser. "I know I'm a bit messy and my taste is all over the place."

The shifter sounded self-conscious and Maggie felt bad. "No, it's not that at all. I don't know many shifters—or any—and I was just wondering how differently they live from humans." There, that didn't sound so horribly humiliating.

A sports bra flew through the air to land on Maggie's pile.

"It's more versatile and quicker to get off when you shift," Kaitlyn explained about the bra choice. She plopped on her bed, resting on her elbow. "Ya know, I didn't even know I was a shifter until a few years ago."

Maggie's head jerked up from her stash. "How is that possible?" She'd at least known she was different and why.

"No one has a clue. I got into trouble one night and *bam*—four legs. It's when I first met your brother. He'd just started dating my best friend." A wicked smile appeared on her face. "Although I don't think 'dating' is what they were doing." She chuckled.

Maggie would love to meet her. Jace found someone, was happy, and had good company like Kaitlyn around him.

"At least they'd understand if you didn't know anything. Porter's reaction every time he learns of another shifter fact I don't know has made me feel like I've committed a crime."

"He's a stubborn one, I can tell." Kaitlyn sat up and put her elbows on her knees. Maggie noticed her tactical belt and all the weapons strapped to her. Kaitlyn's fluid movements blended her gear into her. She wore it well. "Does his reaction bother you because he's some dude who's judging you, or because you have the hots for him and don't want to feel smaller around his big shifter manliness."

Maggie threw the shirt she wasn't going to wear in Kaitlyn's face. Laughing, Kaitlyn snatched it out of the air and folded it neatly. Maggie became aware that she went from zero to friendship with the female. No longer strangers, she was so relieved to have someone to confide in who wasn't vested in her future, just her.

"He's hot, and he claims he's my mate."

Kaitlyn's grin died. "Don't you feel it?"

Do I want to strip down and have dirty, hard sex with him for days on end? Check. *Does it seem like the only air worth breathing is infused with his scent?* Sigh. Yes. *Is it excruciating being away from him and not knowing if he's okay or if he and Jace have ripped each other apart?* Absolutely.

"How I do I know it's not infatuation?"

Because of the way his tongue took her to heights of ecstasy she hadn't known existed.

"You just do, I guess." Kaitlyn shrugged. "I was raised human, too, so maybe I don't know what it feels like either." Her expression seemed…troubled, but it was replaced by reassurance. "Many of the other guys here are mated and they all just knew."

Maggie's concerns about Porter rose to the surface discussing him. "Is Bennett in charge?" Will he fairly investigate Porter?

As if Kaitlyn read her mind, she answered, "He's a good guy, don't worry. He's been at this for a while. Longer than Seamus. But no, he's not the boss. Commander Fitzsimmons is, but he's out in the field." Kaitlyn's signature grin appeared. "You'll get a kick out of their mates, though."

"What about Chayton?"

Kaitlyn's grin faded and her disquiet returned.

"He's…uh…he'll be fair." She rose and went to the closet to throw her shirt back in. Maggie heard a faint, "While he's being a giant prick."

If Chayton wasn't high on Kaitlyn's likeable list, Maggie didn't know if she wanted the guy responsible for Porter's fate.

"Why don't you like him?"

"Whaaat? Is it obvious?" Kaitlyn's falsetto laced with sarcasm. She kicked the clothes spilling out back enough so she could shut her closet door. "Take how inadequate you feel around Porter, multiply by a hundred, and add in that I'm not jumping into bed with him."

"Because of how you were raised? Is that why he's a dick?"

"It's my best guess."

They both cocked their head to listen to a dull thudding on the porch.

"I recognize Jace's shitkickers. Get changed while I let him in."

Maggie nodded numbly. She shed Bennett's shirt and the oversized sweats and pulled on Kaitlyn's loaners. She felt human again, which might be a sin in this place.

Facing the door to the bedroom, she squared her shoulders and marched out.

She found Jace at the table. Kaitlyn was nowhere to be seen.

"She went to hang out with Cassie so we could talk," Jace's tone suggested he looked forward to their talk as much as she did.

A glass of water and a sandwich sat across from him. Her stomach growled. She plopped down and dug in. It gave her hands something to do while she spoke. "I know I'm sorry doesn't cover it Jace. I wish I could go back, visit you in prison, or at least write a damn letter." She ripped into the stack of meat wedged between two thin slices of bread, and talked around her mouthful. "I mean, I felt so guilty, so dirty, for just cutting you off after you gave everything up for me. I should've just confronted Ma, told her no way I was cutting you out of my life. Told her what she did was wrong. But instead I took the easy way out and caved to everything she wanted. It's been that way my whole life, always what she—"

"Maggie."

She quit talking, stopped chewing altogether, and stared at her brother. His mouth twisted with a bemused smile.

"I can't say I'm okay with it," he began, speaking slowly, considering his words, "but…I understand. You were just a kid."

Maggie dropped her gaze to the empty plate. "I've been an adult for over a decade."

"You still had to rely on her for resources. Did you go to college?"

She nodded. "She pushed me toward a career where I'd only be around humans, and not a lot of them. I'm a preschool teacher at a daycare," she said wryly.

"Sounds Ma's speed."

~131~

"There's things she doesn't know, though."
Jace raised a brow. She took a deep breath, and
spilled her secrets. "That night I was attacked, I
grew up a lot. I was angry about everything.
Enraged and I had no outlet. Then one night when I
was a senior in college, I was walking home and I
saw a guy stalking a girl. I beat the shit out of him
and left him lying in the weeds." Both of Jace's
brows rose. "I started hunting them. It's
my...hobby."

"Your hobby is tracking down human
perverts to beat up?"

She nodded.

"You've never been caught?"

"No. I had a couple of close calls, but I used
my shifter resources." The ones she knew about,
anyway.

"Cool."

"I worked at novelty sex shop thinking I
could find them easier." He dipped his head in
agreement. "Enough pervs came in to keep me
busy."

"I'll bet."

His easy acceptance calmed her, but fueled
her guilt.

"I was strong enough to do that, but not to
track you down."

"It's done," he said. "Besides, with Sigma
around, I would've feared you'd be a target just
associating with me."

"Sigma?"

He glanced at her in surprise, then realization. "Evil organization that hunted shifters and vampires for nefarious reasons. Cassie and I were their targets once. The Guardians helped save us." He lifted his hands as if to say, *And here I am*.

"Are they still around?" She was both scared they still existed, and thrilled to think there was a whole organization of villains she could target.

Whoa. She'd just fought some humans. Why was she thinking an upgrade in prey was warranted?

"Calm down, tiger," he chuckled. "They were destroyed over a year ago. We have a new government."

"Wait! I know this one. The TriSpecies Synod."

"They're slowly transitioning our people to a more democratic society, to keep occurrences like Lobo Springs from happening, keep our kind from drawing attention."

"Since they're transitioning, shifters like Seamus don't have to follow their suggestions?"

Jace thought a moment before answering. "Yes, not yet."

"You don't think Porter's innocent, do you?"

"He's likely correct about Seamus, but his priority is not you." He delivered the statement like a warning and yeah, she'd come to that difficult conclusion, too.

As his mate, it should piss her off, incite raging jealousy, or something other than the conflicted feelings wrestling within her. To make a decision about them, about her future, she needed more information.

"I should talk with him. Where is he?"

"In a cell." Jace's tone was anything but apologetic.

"What?" She pushed back from the table, her instinct to rush to her mate.

"We can't treat him like a guest while we keep Brutus and Cletus locked up."

"I need to talk to him."

"Maggie, that's not a good—"

"I know you don't think so. Think about it. I haven't spent much time with him. He's supposed to be my life partner. I really should just get to know him."

Jace contemplated her request. His eyes, while drilled into the wall, developed a faraway look. "Fine, but we'll have to lock you in with him."

"Did you just mentally talk to someone?" she asked in awe. "We can do that without being in shifter form?"

He nodded.

"Duuude." Her mom! "Have you tried with Ma?"

He nodded once.

Her heart sank. "She's in trouble."

"She's crafty. Don't give up hope."

"That's what Porter said."

Jace snorted softly. "He'd know her better than me, honestly."

"You're right. He grew up under Dad's reign." They both fell silent. Maggie had to ask, "Do you remember him? Or Keve?"

"A little. Dad's eyes were freakier than mine, but he wasn't cruel. Tough, but not mean. Keve and I were close, but after I saw him covered in blood, a silver blade through his heart, I don't remember anything else."

"It's more than I remember," she said sadly. "I recall you and Ma arguing about Lobo Springs, but it was still called Great Moon when you left."

"After high school, I hopped on my bike and headed out to find Great Moon. I came back to ask her if it and Lobo Springs were one and the same."

"And things went nuclear."

He frowned. "You weren't supposed to hear that discussion."

"A fight like that is hard to hide in a small house." She drew in a cleansing breath, her blood urging her to leave the cabin and head to the lodge. "Can you take me to Porter now?"

Chapter Eight

Porter stretched out on the tiny cot, hands behind his head. Tired, but too wired to drift off, his mind worked all the angles: the missing Armana, his mate's lack of enthusiasm regarding him, her brother's coldness toward her, and Brutus' claims of murder.

Lost in thought, it wasn't until his cock twitched that he noticed Maggie's scent wafting over him. Was it his imagination or did she smell stronger, more shifter-like? Lavender and vanilla and, he inhaled again, moonlight. His mother used to have a lavender bed outside of their house. Porter had kept it going, until his lack of a green thumb killed every plant off. Maggie was like a resurrection of his failure, another chance to save the flowers.

Since he sensed Jace, too, he didn't sit up. Jace wouldn't let him see her. The clank of the door's lock grabbed his attention. Maggie stepped in and the door shut behind her with Jace on the other side looking like a father sending his daughter off with her first date.

He swung his legs over the edge and stood. "What's wrong?"

"I asked to come talk to you." She wore a grey and pink tee with snug jeans and brand new shoes. He loved the sex kitten at The Gift Shop look, but casual fit Maggie.

"FYI," Jace grumbled, "you're being watched." He pointed to the cameras in Porter's cell that left little to no privacy.

Talking was all they'd be doing. His body protested, but he wouldn't compromise Maggie like that.

"G'night, Jace." Maggie smiled reassuringly at her brother, who left after a final glare toward Porter.

Porter gestured toward the cot for Maggie to sit. "Everything okay between you and him?"

She settled on top of the blankets, her back against the wall, knees drawn up. "It will be, I think. He doesn't despise me, more hurt and disappointed. I'm not sure about him and Ma. It'll take a lot more than one talk. We'll need time."

"Any word on your mom?"

"He and Kaitlyn are heading out to look for her now."

"Good." He seated himself next to her. Close, but not enough to make his brain short out and turn him into a voyeur. "What'd you want to talk to me about?"

"Stuff."

He pulled a knee up to drape his arm over so he could angle himself toward her. Lavender and vanilla tickled his nose. Fading sunlight from the tiny window close to the ceiling cast her face in shadows, her strong features mysterious, ethereal.

Again, he marveled over what a lucky idiot he was. He'd found his mate, she happened to be the trump card for him, and she was gorgeous.

"Like what?" he prompted.

"Ummm…what's your favorite color?"

What?

She saw the look on his face and burst out laughing. "This is called 'getting to know each other.' Don't shifters do that?"

"Not really. If we want to have sex, we do it, but we know that it's only temporary. Everything is saved for our mates, and even then…well, we're mates." So why bother?

She didn't seem pleased with his answer, and damn if that didn't distress him.

"Wood."

She glanced at him in surprise.

"My favorite color," he explained. "Wood. It's easy on the eyes. Not too bright, not too plain. Depending on the type, the hue can vary, but it's all a shade of brown. I love the smell more, especially freshly cut lumber. Speaking of smell, I built a deck for some family friends out of cedar. There's nothing like the smell of cedar. I'm planning on building myself a deck out of cedar one day."

"I've never smelled cedar," Maggie admitted, like she didn't think it was a confession she'd ever be making. "My favorite color is purple. A lighter purple, but not too light."

Porter lips twitched. "Like lavender."

She swatted his leg with approval. "Exactly."

Grabbing her hand, feeling only brief resistance from her, he twined his fingers through hers and laid them on his leg.

"Favorite movie?" she asked, her voice dropping an octave. He wasn't the only one suffering from restraint.

"I don't watch TV."

"Get the fuck out!"

"I don't own one."

Her eyes grew wide. Is this what she experienced every time she revealed her incomprehension of shifter ways to him? Because it was a little unnerving.

"I was so sheltered, I don't how I would've survived without it. Even when we couldn't afford cable, we got the basic channels. That crosses the next few questions off. Hobbies?"

"Wood."

"You got a thing for it, huh?"

"It's my ability." And she wouldn't know about any of that, either. "We all have a special talent. It's mentally originated, not like a super power. Mine is woodworking. It's why Seamus wouldn't allow me near the job sites he sabotaged. I'd know exactly what happened."

"I have an ability?"

He caressed her hand with his thumb. "Yes, but it may take time to develop while you hone your shifter skills."

They fell quiet. She scooted closer to him, until her head lay on his shoulder. He continued stroking her hand, relaxing them both, yet working each of them up until arousal clogged the room.

Maggie cleared her throat, attempting to sound normal. "What was your childhood like? Or, your whole life before the attack?"

"It was…normal." He wanted to say a normal shifter life, but she wouldn't have any comparison. "We ran wild, went to school, ran the woods on two legs until we transitioned, then we tore through them on four. We were taught about the world, how we need to hide. Back then the colony wasn't well off financially, but we had all we needed."

Until Seamus had taken over. Everything Seamus did was a show and he maintained all the control. They were becoming more isolated and more dependent on their leader.

"Your sister, how old was she?"

A cherubic face drenched in drool haunted Porter's dreams. There was a catch in his voice when he said, "She was ten months old."

Maggie squeezed his hand, snuggling in closer. Her warmth filled up the cold empty place his loved ones' deaths left behind. "What was her name?"

"Angie."

"I'm sorry."

"I know." He dropped a kiss on her head. She rocked into him, the hard wall at their backs. He didn't want their conversation to keep careening into the depressing. "We'd be more comfortable if we stretched out."

She raised her head. "I should go."

"Where?"

Blinking, she frowned. "I don't know."

Tipping her chin up, he whispered, "Stay with me." Her eyes flicked toward a camera. "I promise I won't give them a show. Jace is searching for your mom, we aren't allowed to help with anything else, but we can rest up for what tomorrow brings."

She gazed deeply into his eyes, her blue irises glinting in the darkness. "I'll stay."

Stretching them out, he wrestled the blanket over them. It wasn't cold, their heat would've been enough, but just in case his hands rested...somewhere personal...no one needed to see.

She cuddled into him, and when she looked up say goodnight, he caught her mouth. And groaned. His lips on hers. That's all it was. Her taste had grown stronger, more intoxicating. He didn't have to coax her mouth open, she opened eagerly seeking more contact.

He wanted to plunder her mouth, strip her down under their threadbare covers, release himself to push inside.

But he wouldn't.

She came to him tonight to get to know him. So he'd keep skin-on-skin contact above the neckline, preserve their make-out session to nothing past first base.

Maybe a little groping.

Cradling her head to him with one arm, he used the other to hug her closer. The sweatpants he wore were fortunate for his erection, but his manhood still ached painfully. He resisted rocking his hips into her lest he lose his ever-loving mind in her delicious curves.

Her hand crept down between them, going right for ground zero. Porter snatched it into his and held it close to his chest.

She broke the kiss, her expression confused.

"I want tonight to be about you and me, but it's you, me, and the cameras. If you touch me anywhere near my pelvis, I'm afraid I'll go wild."

The slight twist of her lips revealed her feminine satisfaction of the power she held over him.

Two could play that game.

Deepening the kiss, he swiped his tongue sensually across hers, caressing the sensitive surface, stroking it in the same way he'd lick her center. She stilled, the only movement her hand tightening around his and her tongue meeting each caress. Her body melted completely into him. He wouldn't able to tell where he stopped and she started except his cock made it clear there was a boundary it could not cross.

A slight rocking of her hips drained his best intentions. Frantically, he mentally defeated every reason he had for not tearing their clothes off.

Maggie pulled away with a gasp, her body shuddering faintly within his arms. "If we keep this up, I'm going to implode. Or get myself off if you won't."

He groaned at the lust that shot through his body, making his balls cobalt blue. "I'll keep doing it so I can watch."

She giggled, burrowing into him, tucking her head under his chin. "We should get some sleep."

"It'll be *so easy* with all my blood pooled in one area."

Her legs scissored together, small back and forth movements causing her body to wiggle tantalizingly. "You're not the only one uncomfortable."

His turn for a satisfied grin. "Let's talk. Discussing The Gift Shop is out of the question. I don't need those images in my head. How about why you work with kids?"

Her lashes fluttered against his neck, not expecting the subject change. "Ma's influence, like always. A work environment that shouldn't put me in harm's way; daycares aren't frequented by supernaturals. Deeper into the human world I went."

"Did you like it?"

She rolled a shoulder. "Yes and no. Kids are a blast, but I felt like I had too much energy. It made me popular with the parents—I ran the shit outta their kids." He chuckled, but she grew quiet, pensive.

"Talk to me Maggie."

"It just hit me how glad I am to be done with all that. No matter what happens, I won't have to go back to appeasing Ma and trying to ignore that I'm different. I can finally be *me*. Here I am, cuddled inside, glad I don't have to sneak around anymore, while she might be in danger."

He stroked her back, seeking to comfort his mate. "It's all right to feel that way, Maggie. You can be relieved, you can be pissed at her—it doesn't change how much she means to you."

He must've brought some degree of comfort to her because she relaxed further beside him, as if some weight had lifted. But he knew some guilt remained and she changed the subject. "Now you tell me, why carpentry? Because it's your ability?"

"Most definitely. My dad had the same talent. In a poor colony, surrounded by woods, we were in high demand because we could find all we needed around us and make it into anything. The repairs around town alone would've made us popular. It was crucial the residents not have to buy new every time a piece of furniture busted, or a hormone-raged teen punched a hole in the wall."

"What was your mother's talent?"

Porter turned onto his back, pulling Maggie into his side, her head resting on his shoulder. "Plants. Not terribly useful in a community of meat eaters, but she grew the most beautiful flowers."

They lay, encompassed in their private shell of warmth.

"I wish I knew my dad," she said faintly. "And Keve."

He had no reply. He yearned to know his baby sister, witness the female she would've grown up to be. They were gone. Instead of words, he dropped a kiss on top of her head, and they remained quiet until they both drifted off to sleep.

***

Armana sat in her car, pulled off into a desolate stretch of road, darkness covering her location. She had no idea where the Guardian headquarters was and it didn't matter. Plans had changed. She'd hidden long enough. Jace was a Guardian, and Mage was grown with a worthy shifter male by her side. More than she could have ever hoped after that late night fleeing with two small children.

Seamus was a dirty bastard. A despicable, cold-hearted, power-obsessed male. Her mate's body hadn't yet cooled when Seamus had shown up. A Cheshire grin on his face, he'd stood over her sleeping children.

"You'll mate with me and I *will* rule," he'd said.

She'd replied with a more vulgar version of "no thank you."

His eyes had flicked down to the bed. "They weren't supposed to survive. You're a more formidable fighter than I expected. Be warned, if you resist me, there's always another way." His eyes slid to the small form of Mage.

His meaning had dawned on Armana. Her body went cold, time-slowed, and she studied the diabolical male in front of her. Seamus had risen to clan leader, often clashing with her mate on how to rule. Their colony was poor, Bane meticulously worked to increase prosperity, incorporate technology, prepare the clans that made up Great Moon for the twenty-first century. It wasn't that Seamus had disagreed, he'd just wanted monopoly over the other clan leaders. Bane hadn't trusted him and neither had Armana.

After that night, her fear of him had been her motivation. She was terrified she'd lose her surviving children. Seamus' brand of evil—she couldn't compete with. Sigma agents had attacked Great Moon, tearing through families, until they were driven back, and it had all been due to Seamus' manipulations. The scenario spelled out more trouble than she could comprehend. Seamus had made a deal with the biggest enemy her people had ever faced. Not just their centuries-long grudge with vampires, these were the most nefarious of even them.

So she'd fled and dealt with the cowardly guilt ever since. At the time, she didn't know how she'd survive each night. She'd wanted to lay down with her mate, tear her own heart out performing rites for her oldest boy, but she had Jace and Mage. Seamus' late night visit completed her reason for living.

If she could've escaped across the country, she would've. But she'd only been able to make it to Freemont. Not ideal as it was the closest city to Great Moon, but it was populated enough that they got lost within its limits. The women's shelter accepted them, helped her find work. She saved enough money to pay for fake documents for all of them from a contact she'd heard Bane refer to frequently. And she'd cut ties completely with her people, shedding her scent and absorbing the human aroma that accompanied her lack of shifting and living in an urban area.

Should she have done things differently? Probably. Attacked Seamus as he stood there with that mocking grin on his face. Yelled for help. Gone to the other clan leaders and reported him. Found sanctuary with the Guardians.

As much as she questioned her actions, she had to remember there was a significant con for each one. She was strong, Seamus more so. Each family in the colony was lost in their own grief;

help may not have answered her cries. Seamus had proven his influence was far reaching. No telling how much he corrupted those who lived close by. As for locating the Guardians, she'd barely made it to the city. Finding their quasi-hidden location proved too much for her and Seamus would know she'd left by then and taken measures to prevent her from locating them.

Armana sighed and stepped out of her car. She'd never allowed herself to live in the past, but tonight was different. Tonight, she faced it.

Her shirt came off and drifted to the ground. Next she shucked her shoes and pants. Mentally, she calculated the years since she'd last shifted. Almost twenty-five. Not even when she'd squirreled Jace to a rural spot for his first shift had she transitioned. She'd only allowed him to transition once before they went back to town, and she fretted he'd get sniffed out by other shifters. She wouldn't have done it at all, but raising a teenage boy was tough. The aggression of his genetics created more problems for her.

Mage had gotten a free pass. Always a mellow kid, she was more compliant after the trauma she'd suffered at the hands of that rapist. Truth was, if Jace hadn't killed that man, she didn't know that she wouldn't have, ripping the man apart while pretending he was Seamus.

Trading one kid for another was not a decision any parent should have to make. Keeping tabs on him hadn't been an option. Too risky, too much a threat to Maggie. She hated Seamus all the more for putting her in that position, even as she despised herself more. Jace's strength and resourcefulness had always been apparent, and she had trusted in those traits to carry him through. They had and now it was time for Armana to return to where it had all began.

Instinct flooded back. Her senses grew sharper, clearer, and her rage at what happened, long suppressed, was finally allowed to crest. She spun around, like she was chasing her tail. For a second, she felt like she was being watched. Overreaction after years of suppressing her full potential.

Fangs bared, the image of Seamus and his cruel green eyes in her head, she hunted.

Chapter Nine

M aggie's eyes flew open with a gasp. Porter jerked awake, mumbling a sleepy, "What is it?"

"I saw Ma. I knew everything she was thinking." She scrambled off the cot to bang on the door.

"Maggie, it's the middle of the night. Calm down and tell me what you saw first."

Pounding once more, she peered into the camera. "I know where my mom is.

"At first I thought I was dreaming, but it seemed so *real*. I could *hear* her thoughts. I know why we left all those years ago." Maggie spun toward a bewildered Porter. "Seamus was behind the attack."

Understanding dawned in his features, he nodded like it all made perfect sense and it did. It all did.

She concentrated. *Jace!*

Maggie?

Yes, it worked! *I know where Ma is. I mean, I don't know, but I can find the area.*

How?

Her excitement died. Would they believe her? Porter seemed to accept it, but he'd believe Seamus was the devil if she told him. *I dreamed it.*

Have you dreamed like this before? Jace asked.

Never.

Where is she?

Maggie stalled, slanting a glance at Porter. He waited as if sensing she was mentally communicating. At least she wasn't broadcasting the conversation like earlier.

Maggie, where is she? What did it look like?

She could tell him in intricate detail, but then she'd be left to fret here. *I'll tell you when you pick us up.*

Fuck, Maggie, where is she?

I don't know, I only saw it. But Maggie knew where she was going.

Be right there.

She turned to a patient Porter. "Jace and Kaitlyn must be out searching the area around here. They're coming back."

"Did you tell him where Armana is?"

Maggie couldn't help the wry smile twisting her lips. "I said I'd tell him more when he came and got us."

Warmth infused Porter's eyes. "That's my girl."

Someone entered at the end of the corridor. Maggie bounced up and down waiting. Mercury stopped at the door, holding Porter's paint-splattered clothing. Maggie's items were tucked inside.

He dumped them on the floor, a grumpy expression on his face. From his bone-weary features, his unpleasant disposition wasn't due to her or Porter. The depth of fatigue she sensed from him originated long before they had arrived. These Guardians fascinated her in a way she couldn't explain. She wanted to know more about them, but her mother took preference.

"Get changed. I'll be right outside the door."

"The Guardians and their hospitality." Porter stooped, picking up the pile. "I'll turn my back." He sounded as disgruntled as Mercury looked.

She'd turn around, too, because a nude Porter was more than distracting, and they were running out of time.

He pivoted when he heard her tying her shoes. "Ready."

"More than." Anticipation sang through her nerves. It was the same feeling she got when she tracked pervs through the streets and clubs of Freemont.

There was no going back to her previous way of life. No more novelty store, no more daycare. The last few years, she'd wanted to crawl out of her skin. Now she could because she had an alternate form. She had an ability. She didn't understand it one iota, but her special shifter skill was dream...something. Scrying? Dream scrying. Yeah, she liked that.

They exited the corridor. Mercury had been resting against the wall with his eyes closed, but he was already heading down another hallway. Winding through the lodge, they went up a set of stairs and out the front door where her brother and Kaitlyn waited by a black SUV. Another male stood next to them.

If Maggie thought any of the other Guardians she'd met were imposing, this guy made them seem like puppies. Confidence and power radiated from him. His hazel eyes reflected a predatory gleam in the dark, his ruddy appearance indicated no softness.

"Maggie," Jace spoke, "this is my boss, Commander Fitzsimmons. Tell him what you told me, only," he threw her a warning glance, "tell him everything."

Porter grabbed her hand. Grateful for his comfort, she peeked up at him. Calmly he gazed at the commander, wary, but not distrustful. Did she look like that, or did she look like a deer facing an eighteen wheeler?

On her other side, Mercury rubbed his eyes, uncaring about the situation.

"Mercury," the commander's voice was quiet, packed full of authority, but there was no sign of cruelty, "go home, get some sleep."

The male snorted. "Doubt it. As soon as I lay down, the twins' eyes will pop open." He trudged away.

"How old?" Maggie murmured. She wasn't sure they'd trust her with an answer.

"Newborns." The commander's expression softened, as if he found Mercury's situation humorous, but he felt for the guy.

Maggie often helped in the baby room. They were cute, they were precious, but they were ruthless, lacked empathy, and would completely destroy a person's stamina, Guardian or not. She sympathized, too.

"Tell me what you saw." Commander Fitzsimmons' attention turned back to her. It was like Porter wasn't there, only she doubted the commander missed anything.

"I dreamed it all." She prepared for disbelief as she told her story. But like Jace, he readily accepted her tale.

"Has anything like this happened before?" he asked.

She shook her head. "Nothing."

"And you've lived around humans your whole life, shifting only for the first time yesterday?"

"Yep." Of course, he'd been advised of her circumstances.

"You're a dream walker, only your target doesn't need to be asleep the same time as you. It's rare."

Jace inspected her like a bug in a jar. Great. She reclaimed her shifter-hood and she turned out to be an oddity. "Dream walking is rare, or me peeking in on thoughts of totally conscious people?"

"Both, but the latter is extremely rare." He directed his attention to Jace. "You'll need to head out right away. Bring Chayton. Kaitlyn, head to Armana's house and look for evidence of Seamus or any other intrusion."

A sharp inhale escaped Kaitlyn, but she remained quiet. Maggie wondered if it was an insult to switch partners.

Jace rounded the SUV to get into the driver's seat. Maggie stepped forward so abruptly, she yanked Porter along, still clutching his hand. "I want to go."

"We *both* do," Porter added.

"I don't think so," an unfamiliar voice said behind her.

She whipped around to a tall, lanky male exiting the lodge. He wore arrogance like a badge. His hair was ink black and hung in a long braid down his back, his eyes the color of rich coffee, and his stature compared to the burly shifters around her was slender, but he'd still outmuscle a human. From the displeasure emanating from Kaitlyn, she determined this male to be Chayton.

He breezed past her and Porter, ignoring their presence, and climbed into the passenger side. No, he wasn't discounting them, he was too busy glowering at Kaitlyn, who actively pretended he didn't exist.

He wasn't in charge, so Maggie couldn't care less about his opinion. "Commander," she beseeched, "I *need* to look for my mother."

Something in her tone stopped the commander. She held her breath as he considered her request. Jace had already hopped into the vehicle, confident she'd be denied. Chayton's window lowered, both males waiting for the commander's answer.

Commander Fitzsimmons' eyes narrowed on her and he inhaled deeply. Released it, inhaled again, exhaling through his mouth.

"Go ahead, but listen to Jace. He's taking lead."

Jace and Chayton were both arguing when the commander cut them a look that ceased all talk. Kaitlyn smirked at the pissed off male in the passenger seat.

Maggie ran to dive into the backseat, Porter right behind her.

***

After hours of driving to reach the outskirts of Lobo Springs and canvassing the area to find where Maggie saw Armana hide the car, they finally located the abandoned vehicle in late afternoon. To Porter, it was several hours too late. He was starving for Maggie, sitting that close to her and not being able to touch her confused his cock, especially after abstaining from her body's paradise during the night. With two other males in the vehicle, one being her brother, trying to ignore his discomfort should've been easy…if it wasn't for his mate just inches away.

Then there was Chayton's bitching. And his nickname for Porter.

"I'll stay with Maggie; you go with Chayton." Jace motioned in an arc encompassing the woods around them. "We'll spread out, following each side of my mother's trail. Stay downwind, don't try to contact her. If she's in a tight spot, I don't want to startle her. If Seamus has her, I don't want him to sense we're near."

Maggie vibrated with energy next to Porter. He hated parting with her, especially this close to Seamus, but like Chayton had pointed out on their ride—several times—he wasn't armed. Having her go with Jace stirred a less homicidal rage than imagining her at the mercy of an dick like Chayton. He didn't doubt she could handle herself, it was the principle that she shouldn't have to.

Before they began, Jace circled to the back of the SUV and opened up the hatch.

Chayton shook his head in disbelief. "Seriously. These guys are going to get us shot."

Jace ignored him like he'd been doing the entire ride and pulled out two handguns. He checked them out, ensured they had full magazines and handed one over to Porter. "Know how to use one?"

It'd been awhile, but he did. His dad had made sure he could shoot, use knives, whatever was needed to defend himself and his people. Porter secured it in his waistband, the solid metal settling against his back. He'd rather use his hands to build, not destroy, but to protect Maggie and his colony…

Jace was giving Maggie a quick rundown in gun use and safety when Chayton swatted his shoulder. "Let's go, Lumberjack."

Porter rolled his eyes toward the infuriating male, but he'd already taken off at a swift trot. After checking on Maggie, Porter took off after him.

Running through the trees was much less challenging on four legs. The heavy work boots Porter wore weren't made for being fleet of foot. Chayton's black shitkickers looked wicked thick, but the sole resembled a tennis shoe more than a boot—shitrunners.

Armana's scent hung in the air, its shifter element growing stronger. She'd parked several miles away from Lobo Springs, knowing residents dotted the countryside, their small houses hidden among the trees. Only rough dirt trails cut through the woods to each dwelling, their county not affluent enough to build decent roads. Many shifters had preferred it that way, but times were changing and they wanted to adapt with it.

He strained to hear Maggie and Jace, but picked up nothing. He would expect that from Jace, but for Maggie to be as stealthy was unusual. Perhaps because she was more comfortable on two legs. She'd wanted to shift again, badly. The excitement poured off her, but popping up naked to face Seamus wouldn't be very effective. With her body, it might be the distraction the Guardians needed to take him down.

Chayton slowed to a stop, his eyes narrowed, searching through the brush. He held up a hand for Porter to be quiet—like he was being a chatty fucker who tromped around while Chayton concentrated. The guy was a prick.

Catching his breath, Porter opened his mind up to his surroundings.

Where had Armana's scent gone?

They were only a mile away from the edge of town. With her anger, her desire to destroy Seamus, it should be easy to pick up on her trail.

"Where the hell…?" Chayton trailed off. He bent down. Any farther, he'd have his nose to the ground like a bloodhound. He squatted down, squinting into the distance. "She's out for blood. Lumberjack, if you were a bitter mom finally free to exact revenge and terminate the threat to your daughter, where would you go?"

It was Monday, mid-morning. Porter would be at a job site, already busy. What would Seamus be doing?

Lots of secretive meetings. Wandering up and down Main Street, stopping in to chat with all the influential shifters who were under his control.

Insinuating his power onto those who'd resisted so far.

"She would stalk him." Porter pointed to the general areas he was addressing. "He'd be downtown. For lunch, he eats out, planning who he'll bed at night, then he goes to his office, which is his home."

Seamus' house sat on the highest point in town, so he could monitor everything. The previous owner had lived there his whole life, since before Great Moon was established. He'd been a hermit who'd died of old age, but now, Porter doubted his death was natural.

"Exciting guy," Chayton said dryly. "Assuming Armana doesn't know his schedule, she'll follow him if she can remain undetected, and from the absence of her scent, I'd say she's succeeding."

"You think she can hide herself at will?"

"Seen it before," Chayton slipped into mind speak with Jace, keeping him and Maggie in on the conveyance. *Let me guess, you lost her scent?*

You, too? Jace asked.

She ghosted. Did you know she could do that?

No, but it explains how she got away from him and remained unfound.

Lumberjack says he should be heading home about now. My guess is Armana will be lying in wait. She'll probably assume his thugs are still searching for Maggie. It'd be a good time to strike.

Jace disappeared from his head, probably to speak to Maggie who was staying out of their heads, unwilling to risk missing the mental mark and notify Seamus they'd arrived.

Head to his place, Jace ordered. *We'll follow your trail there since we don't know where his residence is.*

Roger. Chayton ushered Porter ahead of him. "I need you to lead the way, Paul Bunyan."

"The thing about nicknames," Porter mused, "is that once you're nailed with an awful one, it makes the rest sound good. Stick to Lumberjack."

Chayton grinned, revealing even white teeth, his fangs concealed. "When you wear a red plaid flannel shirt, it just inspires so many."

He'd retort "chicks dig it," but Maggie hadn't exactly fallen all over him. He trudged ahead, thinking how the ordeal of the last two-and-a-half decades was coming to a head and it'd all be over soon.

She didn't throw herself at him, but they'd connected, resting in each other's embrace on his cot. Maggie reconciled with her family, there were no more secrets, and she was going back home. His home. Where she belonged.

With no sign of Armana, they crept closer to Seamus' house. The growth around them grew sparser. They stayed low, darting from tree to tree. The thinner the trees got, the riskier it became. Porter took off his red shirt to not be noticed, leaving it at the base of a tree. The incline of the land increased with each step, but they were close, could see it. The large three story structure had been renovated—not by Porter—since Seamus had lived in it. It exuded stately elegance, but failed to hide the filth inside.

He sensed Maggie before Jace, his body so attuned to her. Glancing back, he caught her eye just before a crash and a male's shout ripped through the air.

"Stay here!" Chayton sprinted toward the noise emanating from the inside of Seamus' house.

Jace raced past him after ordering Maggie to stay put. She didn't listen. Porter grabbed her arm as she ran by, but she slipped through.

He had no choice to but to go after her.
Maggie, let them to do their job!

Ma's in there.

Maggie!

The sounds of struggle grew stronger, snarls of rage permeated the air. At least one of the combatants was a wolf.

Chayton dived through a first floor window, shattering it on impact. Jace darted around the side, to the front entrance. Maggie skidded to a stop under the window Chayton had plowed through. Grabbing the ledge with both hands, she hauled herself up, glass cutting into her palms.

"Ma! Stand down," Jace ordered from inside.

Muffled snarling—Armana's teeth must be sunk into one of Seamus' body parts.

"Get her off me!"

Porter took perverse pleasure in the pain in Seamus' voice.

Warning shouts from the Guardians didn't stop the sounds of scraping glass. Porter's ears formed a picture in his mind of Seamus spinning with a large wolf, trying to shake her loose.

Claws on the floorboards came closer to the window. Maggie swung a knee up to crawl over, her gaze riveted on the struggling pair.

"No!" she cried.

A gun clicked with a whooshing sound unlike any gun Porter had heard before. A heavy body thudded on the floor. Porter didn't have time to react when he heard the fast approaching footsteps, other than to grab Maggie and yank her back into him, twisting to take the brunt of the fall.

"What are you—" Her scream cut off as a large form leapt out the window and took off into the woods.

Porter recognized Seamus' departing form. Chayton leaned out the window, aiming at the male's back. A quick look at the weapon explained the weird noise. It was a dart gun; he intended to tranq Seamus.

Fuck. That.

Porter released Maggie and rolled up, drawing his weapon from his waistband.

It was just like target practice…over a quarter of a century ago.

He centered Seamus in his sights. The male ducked around trees, weaving to keep from getting hit. Seamus twisted around one trunk, Porter aimed for the other side. When the body crossed into his sights, he fired.

Seamus' shoulder jerked, he stumbled in surprise, but continued running. Unwilling to fire randomly into the woodland, Porter waited for another opportunity, but Seamus had gotten too far away.

Chayton leaned out, his gun popped; they all waited in breathless anticipation. Keen eyes watched the dart fly through the air…and fall short two hundred yards from the target.

"These things have shit range," Chayton muttered.

"Ma!" Maggie rose and jumped to the window.

A startled Chayton lunged out of her way as she sailed in; Porter followed.

Once inside, he hated being surrounded by Seamus' tobacco-laced scent. Smoke and asshole, that's what he smelled. A sable-colored wolf lay on her side, out cold. Jace knelt next to her, a hand resting on her pelt.

Maggie eased down next to him, running her hands up and down Armana's side. "She's not hurt."

"She got the jump on Seamus before he could draw his knife or gun." Jace rose, pacing around the room. "Call a town meeting, Porter.

Chayton, go back and grab our ride. And Maggie, what were you thinking?" He turned back to face her, but she was no longer there.

She was snooping through Seamus' items. "Is this his office? I bet he has some kind of trophy for his bad deeds." She rifled through papers, searched drawers, eventually Jace joined her.

A landline phone sat on Seamus' desk. Porter used it to call the other clan leaders individually. They all paused, unwilling to cross Seamus, until Porter informed them that the Guardians would find them and physically drag them to Town Hall.

Jace raised an eyebrow at the threat but didn't deny it.

Papers rustled, furniture was moved, Maggie was relentless in her search for proof against Seamus for his crimes against her family. If he kept any, she would've found them by now.

"I thought I smelled cigarette smoke." She tossed a pack of unfiltered on top of the dresser she rummaged through.

Porter checked the time. They'd have to get to Town Hall soon. "I think him running off when your mother and the Guardians arrived confirms the intention of his actions. Either way, you're here and you trump Seamus' rule."

Movement ceased. The siblings stared at him.

"I'm not taking over," Maggie said. "I need to stay with my mother."

Porter understood her need to ensure her mom was well, but there was no way she'd refuse taking over now that Seamus was on the run while the village was left with no one.

Armana twitched, the first sign she was regaining consciousness, but she still had a ways to go. Maggie was right. When Chayton returned, they couldn't just throw Armana in the back seat with the windows cracked to hang out while the Guardians confronted the clan leaders.

Jace hurriedly texted on his phone. "You've got a place in town, right Denlan?"

"It's on the other side of the colony," as far away from Seamus as he could get, "built into a hillside." He rattled off his address.

"Take Armana and Maggie. Bennett and Kaitlyn are driving up to hunt for Seamus. He's lived here his whole life; he can't have gone too far."

"No," Porter agreed, "we haven't heard the last of him."

He wouldn't be involved with the meeting. It was for the best. It'd help Jace and Chayton seem impartial, give the clan leaders the rundown of what just happened. It'd also give Maggie a chance to immerse herself in Lobo Springs. Give her blood a chance to remember its home and draw her back. Once that happened, there was no way she'd turn her back on Lobo Springs and its shifters.

Stooping down, he slid his arms under Armana, lifting her up until she was settled across

~166~

his shoulders. "Maggie, can you find the keys to Seamus' ride?"

Chapter Ten

Maggie sat in the backseat with her mom, who'd started twitching more. She'd probably shift once she came to. And she'd be naked. Her mom may not mind even after all these years away from shifter life, but Maggie sure would. So she'd pilfered a shirt and shorts from Seamus's stash. After her time at The Gift Shop, she was impressed by his collection of restraints. Digging for shorts, she'd found handcuffs, ball gags, leather ties. Finding basketball shorts had been no easy task for a male who seemed to prefer not to wear clothing around his house.

One hand buried in her mom's fur, she gazed out the window. Proud structures stood, defying the wear of years, and the lack of updates. Porter avoided downtown where she saw taller buildings, many built with brick, much like the older areas in Freemont. Lobo Springs had no towering walls of glass reflecting sunlight. Houses were small, worn down, but not rundown. Proud shifters lived here, they took care of what they had.

Much like Guardian headquarters, Lobo Springs organized itself among nature. Large cottonwoods shaded many structures, the trees clearly having been at the location first. Porter wove through the streets that didn't run straight like Freemont. Like the houses and businesses, the road moved with the land, instead of moving the land for the road.

Around a curve, a good-sized home appeared. Maggie leaned forward.

Is this place for real?

All the log cabins she'd seen—on TV, of course—were square or rectangular. This one curved itself into the gently sloping hillside. The logs were all different shapes, not uniform pieces stacked precisely, but like a puzzle. Large windows ran from end to end across the front, facing the east. She could almost feel the early morning sun, warming her face, gently waking her up after a night spent in Porter's arms.

Well, that thought came out of nowhere.

There was no time to analyze it because Porter pulled into the driveway, parking in front of a two stall garage.

"I'll park this inside in case Seamus gets close to town."

The empty garage reminded Maggie that his vehicle was still parked in the cheap motel's parking lot. Or sat in impound. Or someone stole it.

"I'm sorry about your pickup," she blurted. How many hundreds of dollars in tools did he have stored in the box?

He opened the back door. "Couldn't be helped." When he reached to grab her mother, he snatched his hands back like he'd been burned.

The fur under Maggie's hand turned to smooth skin. The shaggy head resting in her lap became her mom's youthful face.

Armana sat up with a snarl. Porter stepped back and turned around. She doubted he was worried about her mother's modesty, but more about her own reaction to Porter seeing her mother in the buff.

Because her mom and had a rockin' body, and even though she didn't feel jealous in the slightest, it'd just be awkward. Really.

Chest heaving, her mom looked around, calming when she sensed Porter and Maggie.

Putting a hand on her forehead like she could rub away the fuzziness, she asked, "Did Jace knock me out?"

"Another Guardian did." Maggie handed the stolen clothing over. "Seamus got away. Jace is dealing with...clan stuff. We're at Porter's."

Her mom pulled the shirt on, wiggled into the shorts, and then sat with her eyes closed. "Is Jace coming here when he's done?"

"I don't know."

A wave of sadness rolled through the cab. Her mom's blue eyes opened, shining with regret. "I need to explain to both of you what I did."

"Actually… I already know. I dreamed what you were doing last night."

Armana chuckled softly. "Your father could do that." A sad sigh escaped her. "For all the good it did us."

Porter led them inside. His home was rustic, sparse. Nothing hung on the walls, although they were artwork in themselves. Chairs. That was all the furniture he had. Beautiful, handcrafted chairs. Two of them. Was that a sawhorse in the living room?

He followed her gaze. "I told you I don't own a TV. But," he pulled open his fridge door, "I have food."

***

Porter opened the door to let Jace and Chayton in. He sincerely hoped that when they left, they'd take Armana with them. Not because he disliked her, nor because she'd been interrogating him about his past, but because Maggie's scent permeating his house, mingling with his, was driving him feral.

He should thank Armana for distracting him enough that he didn't carry Maggie caveman-style to his bedroom and ravish her. His mate wouldn't have time to protest, though from her furtive glances all afternoon, he suspected she wouldn't.

Armana sat stiffly in a chair while Jace filled them in on the whole lotta nothing they accomplished with the wary clan leaders who still feared Seamus, or supported him. Her eyes roamed Jace's face and evidence of her heartbreak wove into the tension lines around her eyes. They were nothing compared to the pride that radiated off her.

"We're going to stay in town, continue searching for Seamus with the others." Jace scanned around the room, pinning each one of them with his perturbing stare. "*None* of you will enter those woods to search on your own."

"I need to talk with you first, Jace." Armana's hands twisted in her lap.

Maggie's breath froze in her lungs. Porter rested his hand on her shoulder.

"It's a bad time, Ma," Jace said in a carefully measured tone.

"Not really, dude." Chayton was either oblivious to the strained relationship between Jace and Armana, or stupid. More likely, he wanted to instigate. "There's three of us searching now that Bennett and Kaitlyn have arrived. Thanks to Porter, Seamus left us a good blood trail for at least an hour before he healed. We can spare you for an hour or two."

Jace covered his *are you kidding me?* expression quickly, replacing it with a neutral look. "Sure, we can talk."

Armana flattened her palms on her legs, meeting Jace's gaze. "Alone."

Always a mother, her tone brokered no argument.

Jace sighed. "You'll be all right here, Maggie?" Porter took that to mean Jace no longer thought he was the worst thing that'd happened to her. Maggie nodded, not meeting Porter's gaze. "Fine. You can come to the hotel with us."

Porter ushered everyone out of his house and bolted the door. He watched the three shifters load up and leave before he turned to Maggie.

"You and I have some unfinished business."

She licked her lips, driving him insane. That tongue was going to be all over him by the end of the night. Standing, she ran her hands down her pants like they'd gotten clammy.

He advanced on her. She backed up.

"Do you want this?"

"Yes." The throaty quality in her voice drove his lust up another notch. "It just seems so sudden after everything we've been through."

"No, Mage. It's not sudden. It's been excruciatingly drawn out since the moment I walked into that store." His gaze swept her body. "I'd love to see you in a few of those outfits that were on display."

"The store! And work! I forgot to call and tell them I wouldn't be in."

"Call them later," he growled.

Her pupils dilated at his aggression. He smelled her arousal; it was as strong as his own.

"Okay." She rushed him.

He clamped her close to this body, meeting her lips as she smashed them into his.

Yessss.

Shirts ripped, pants were dragged down, they stumbled to step out of them while maintaining contact with their tongues. After several frustrating seconds, she pushed him back to kick her shoes off. He did the same. Damn boots.

Finally, his feet were free and he stepped out of his pants. Maggie was already naked.

The dim light in the cheap motel hinted at her beauty, but the daylight pouring into the room accentuated every curve. Her skin radiated heat, almost glowing with her desire. Porter shrugged the remains of his shirt off and swung her up into his arms.

Her lips trailed his shoulder. When he felt a hint of fang scrap his skin, he quickened his step, his strides eating the distance to his room, his bed.

Foreplay was done. Everything in him screamed to put his mark on her. He was more than obliged to listen.

Laying her down, he caught her legs and splayed them wide. Her folds glistened, his cock straining to reach them, bury itself inside.

Porter tugged on her legs, pulling her toward him. He positioned himself and drove inside.

Her back arched, baring her graceful neck. Her moan of pure bliss mimicking his own.

Nothing had ever felt this good, so right. Her warmth surrounded him, inviting him to seat himself so deeply his balls hit her ass. Her sex clamped tightly around him. Tremors pulsated through her channel and if he didn't start pumping, he'd release from that sensation alone.

Not before she hit her first peak. Even the need to mark his mate bowed down to ensuring her pleasure.

He set an unforgiving pace, but from the sounds emanating from her, there was nothing to forgive.

Her hands trailed down his chest to his abdomen, and back up, her fingernails lightly scoring him. He fucking loved it. Pressing her knees out wide, he aimed for deeper penetration. Maggie's hands fell away, her climax bearing down on her. He held off his own—with great effort—driving her toward satisfaction first.

A tight swirl with his thumb on her clit sent her walls spasming around his tender shaft.

"Oh, Porter!" Her voice ricocheted off the walls.

Maggie, abandoned in sexual pleasure, her breasts bouncing with his thrusts, her legs pushed out wide, was the most mind-blowing image he'd ever seen. He wanted it burned into his retinas, her portrait, his alone to conjure.

His will gave out. The dam of self-control broke, his balls tightened with exquisite pain before the rush of ultimate sensation overrode his body. He clenched, jerked, thrust forward one last time, and emptied himself inside her, groaning her name—her real name.

"You're mine, Mage." he growled.
Releasing her legs, he dropped over her, bracing an arm by her head to prevent himself from collapsing

on her. His own damn legs wanted to give out, but he had plans for them.

He might've just experienced the best orgasm known to shifter-kind, but he wasn't done with Mage Troye.

She needed to be claimed.

He withdrew. Leaving the searing wrap of her body made him shudder. His was still rock hard, anticipating what was coming, he grabbed one of her hips to roll her over. Her eyes drifted open, her gaze landing on his fully erect manhood.

"Again already?" There was a hitch in her question, like she couldn't believe…her luck.

"I ain't no human, baby," he drawled, flipping her over and lifting her hips until her ass was raised in the air. "You'll be saying 'again already' all night."

She stretched, leaning back toward him with a slight wiggle. The temptation astounded him, but he needed to admire the view of her awaiting his mark: rounded, firm ass cheeks, swollen wet center from being well-loved, and an inviting look being thrown over her shoulder.

Picture. Permanent. Every time he closed his eyes, he'd see this erotic fantasy to remind him what a gift she was.

He didn't enter her right away. Lazily sliding a finger from her clit until he entered her, feeling her slick with his release.

"I feel myself inside of you." He pumped his finger in and out, stroking back down to her nub, only to repeat the process.

"Porter, you're driving me crazy."

"That's the point, Mage."

Her hips bucked in a rhythm that urged him to go faster, but he kept it slow, relaxed. He was anything but. The only way he kept from going mad was watching Maggie's body flush, her pants as she strained for more, the tint in her cheeks from her first release.

He wanted her coming when he seated himself inside.

So he played. She twisted, writhed, moaned for him to go faster. He wanted to explode, but he kept it down.

It would be worth it.

Finally, he relented, quickening his pace. She sighed in approval, threw her head back, curving herself into his hand. He worked her tight sex, circled her clit, until he felt her walls clamp his fingers with the first ripples of orgasm.

Removing his hand, he drove inside. He leaned over her back, reaching around to continue stroking her center.

"Porter," she gasped, bucking under his hand, "I can't keep up."

"I've got you Mage. Trust me with your body."

She was strong, her capability to reach epic states of euphoria not yet tapped. His either, but he knew he could reach them with her.

Licking along her shoulder, up her neck, she thrashed under him, her climax unrelenting. He clamped her against him, his hips pistoned, until the crest of his orgasm hit.

Rearing his head back, he bared his fangs and struck the juncture of her neck and shoulder, marking her.

Cries turned to turn wails as Maggie's ecstasy reached cataclysmic levels. Porter knew—her body squeezed his shaft with extreme force, milking every drop from him, way past the point of going dry.

He'd heard rumors of the mark, how it increased the power of the orgasm.

Sweet Mother Earth, his eyes were closed but he saw stars. When his jaw slackened, he realized they both had slumped to their sides, chests heaving, their sweat-slicked bodies still interlocked.

For once, he wasn't hard around Maggie.

Never mind.

He was gaining his wits, meaning his brain registered the naked female in his embrace who carried his mark.

Sexy as hell. Blood pooled back into his shaft, prepping for another bout of eye-crossing orgasms.

Maggie stretched and carefully extracted herself to turn in his arms. "That was unfucking real." She exhaled a boneless sigh, crumpling against him,

"I'll give you a few minutes before I have my way with you again."

"No, Porter," he frowned at her refusal, "you'll wait until I'm rested so I can have my way with you."

Hell yes.

Chapter Eleven

"Like this?" Maggie, wearing only a blue flannel shirt of Porter's, positioned the handsaw.

"Go for it." Porter stood behind her, hands resting on her waist.

She pulled back, skipping the saw over the wood. "Oh, shit."

"Use your strength, don't be timid."

She tried again, this time cutting a nice line through the wood. He angled down to nibble along her neck. Leaning back into him, she finished the cut, dropped the saw, and spun in his arms.

"We just got done," she said between kisses on his chin. "You were supposed to show me what you do for a living."

He caught her mouth, nipping her lip, knowing it drove her *freaking* crazy.

"I'm going to do you for a living." His hard length pressed against her belly through his jeans.

He wore no shirt and she preferred it that way. The bunch of his muscles and the scattering of hair on his broad chest captivated her. To conceal, that was a shame.

"Sounds like a good time." Oh it would be. He'd proven it many times. "But Jace will be here soon and we need to get dressed."

Her brother had met with the other leaders again. After they saw proof with their own eyes that Seamus was gone, albeit temporarily, and heard his three brutes were either dead or had been transported to Synod custody, they'd started talking. They spilled secrets of blackmail and produced evidence of threats held against them and family members. Jace had also put in a request to search Sigma's records that had been obtained by their new government to determine how Seamus had worked with the vile organization.

"I'll let you go." He nipped her ear, sending shivers to places that made her want to squeeze in one last quickie. "This once."

Maggie danced away from him, throwing a teasing grin over her shoulder. He growled and lunged for her. She squealed and sped up, laughing into his bedroom.

He didn't follow her which was good because they'd both end up in bed. Or against the wall. Or in the shower. Again.

She smiled to herself as she sorted out her shirt and pants from the tangle on the floor. She liked him. A lot. After their night together, she went dreamy-eyed whenever she thought about him. The way the tendons in his neck strained as he reared over her, how he grunted her name—her real name—when he came, the way his butt flexed under hands as he drove into her. How talented he was with his hands.

Yeah, she had it bad. And he was a good guy. He worked hard, loved his village, and always made her feel special.

Her stomach fluttered. In several ways.

It was all coming together. Her history had been revealed and her relationship with her brother was on the mend. He and their mom were actually talking. Maggie was discovering her true identity, her shifter capabilities, and she had a wonderful male to do it with.

Her whole life she'd felt incomplete and, for the first time, she imagined herself whole, or as one half of a whole with Porter.

A knock on the front door spurred her into action. She was dressed within minutes and bounding out to see if it was Jace.

It was.

She slowed, not at all liking the heated expressions on Jace and Porter's faces. They spoke quietly, but Jace was shaking his head and Porter was gesturing. He was angry about something. They fell silent when she entered.

Jace cocked his head toward her, his nostrils flaring. Her face went crimson. She was an adult, but having a wall of pheromones greet any visitor who walked through the door just seemed weird. Until she noticed Jace studied her and it had nothing to do with her and Porter.

"What?"

"I just came to update you guys." He gave away nothing about what had been going on behind those ice blue eyes.

Okaaay. "What were you and Porter arguing about?"

"Your boyfriend thinks you should lead Lobo Springs."

Not this again. She glanced at Porter. "I don't want to. I've told you that since we met."

"It's your duty, Maggie," argued Porter. "Just like you and I were destined to be, this place is yours."

Facing Jace again, she asked, "And you were telling him it's a bad idea, Jace?"

"I discussed the options with Commander Fitzsimmons who consulted with the Synod. It's his recommendation that the colony votes in their next leader."

"And like I told Jace," Porter countered, "there's no way to know who we can trust. There's no telling who Seamus corrupted, or who holds such a big grudge they want their chance to rule with an iron fist. Your blood trumps all that."

"We'd give it a few days to settle," Jace explained. "Time for someone else to make their intentions known. Denlan, you're seriously invested in the good of the colony, why don't you run?"

Porter threw his hands up. "Because it's not mine to run. It's Maggie's."

She needed to put the brakes on Porter's thought train, be clear and firm. "Porter, I'm not taking over. Period. I don't even know if I want to move here."

His hands dropped to his hips. He glared at the floor before lifting his blazing gaze to her. "Did last night mean nothing to you?"

"Of course it did, but you've had my future decided since *before* you met me. You keep throwing the word destiny around, but no one decides my destiny but *me*. I'm not leaving one relationship where I was told how to live to dive into another one where nothing's changed!" Her voice had risen until she was shouting.

"I met you when Lobo Springs needed you the most." His volume matched hers. "I've had the colony's best interest in mind my *whole* life and when I met one of its ruling bloodlines, she happened to be my mate. What else would I call it?"

"Selfish!" It was the first word that came to mind and in her opinion, it fit Porter perfectly. "It's *my* life, not yours."

"I'm not the one being selfish! You didn't have to live among the constant terror that Seamus would target you next. *Everyone* here did, and you're abandoning them—for your own reasons."

"My dad was killed. His heir was killed. Maybe that's destiny telling the colony to move on! I'm just discovering who I am. I'd think my *mate* would be supportive, but you've had ulterior motives the whole time."

"Because you belong here!"

Argh! They'd gone full circle and Porter still couldn't get it through his thick, obstinate skull.

"Not necessarily." Jace said, his tone dead serious.

Porter scoffed. "Of course you'd say that. Even after what she did to you?"

Maggie gasped. "How *dare* you throw that in my face."

"Enough!" Jace roared. "I'm saying her scent has grown and developed since she's been reaching her full shifter potential. I'm saying I know why the commander allowed her to join us when we came here for Ma."

Porter's breathing slowed as he took in a measured breath. Maggie wanted to sniff under her arms. What about her smell?

"She has a destiny all right," Jace continued. "One she's been working her way toward even as a human."

Porter's face fell. It was like Jace yanked the fight right outta him.

"That's right, Denlan. She's a Guardian."

Jace drained the fight right out of Maggie, too.

Guardian. Her?

"Born Guardians have a unique scent." Jace could've been talking through a bullhorn, she barely heard him, stuck on the change this meant for her life. "It's so we know and can begin training young. With the growth in population and our people spreading out, the Guardians have recruited shifters who'd be a good fit for the life, like me. But you were born for it." He threw a pointed look to Porter. "Destiny."

"Is that something you want to do, Maggie?" Porter's voice was quiet, the direct opposite to less than a minute ago.

It didn't make her any less angry with him. "*Now* you're asking what I want?"

He winced. Was it dawning on him how obtuse he'd been?

A Guardian. How awesome did that sound? No more sneaking around to hunt degenerates, she'd be trained and given weapons and *it would be her job*. Hunting perps like Wally, watching detective shows, being a Guardian fit. It was her.

Sneaking up on sexual predators was certainly less dangerous than facing down feral shifters like Seamus, but her soul rejoiced at the danger. For the first time, her life had a purpose and she knew what it was. She knew who she was. Her life had detoured all those years ago, but Mage Troye's birthright would be fulfilled.

Her delight poured through room. Porter dropped his head in defeat.

"What does that entail?" Her anger at Porter hadn't quite dissipated. He'd get over it. Once he accepted his mate was a badass Guardian!

"We'd train you and then assign you to a section in the area. It might not even be with the West Creek pack."

~186~

Her gaze flew up to Porter, who refused to lift his off the floor. It had to be a shock for him, and she was still pissed about his behavior, but he'd come to accept the news and be thrilled for her.

"When do I start?" She'd call her two employers, out of courtesy only, to tell them they'd never see her again. Giving up her apartment was next, selling her car. Would she get a SUV like a Denali or a Yukon with just shy of legally tinted windows?

That was it. She had no more ties to her old way of life. Not even to Freemont unless her mother went back, but she doubted it.

Jace cut into her ponderings. "I'm heading back today, with Ma, until she decides what she's going to do."

A grin broke out. She wanted to jump up and down and squeal, but she was pushing her thirties and going into law enforcement. Play it cool, play it cool.

His jaw set, Porter still hadn't raised his stare off the floor.

"Porter?"

When he did, she wished he hadn't. Hit with loss and anguish, she struggled to make sense of the emotions pouring off of him.

"My place is here, Maggie."

"I don't understand, Porter. I'm not asking you to move today." But if he didn't accompany her…she didn't know what that meant for them.

"Without you, I'm going to *have* to step in. Encourage the vote...and put myself on the ballot. Seamus is still out there; the colony is vulnerable."

Was...was he breaking up with her? "What about us?"

His expression hardened. "You've made it clear you want nothing to do with my home, and I can't leave. I don't see how there can be an *us*."

Stunned. His declaration hung between. They'd only had a fight, how could he just give up?

Jace gently pulled her toward the door by her elbow. Her feet moved, but her brain had checked out.

"Goodbye, Mage." The sorrow in Porter's words crumbled her already broken heart.

Chapter Twelve

One month later…

"Come on Maggie. Watch your left side." Jace feinted again.

Maggie twisted to protect that side of her abdomen. Jace lashed out, nailing her in the right flank instead. She flew back on the mats, rolled backward, and jumped up into a fighting stance, but Jace stood with his arms crossed, wearing a frown.

She relaxed and blew a stray strand of hair out of her face. Her braid contained most of her thick mane, but some always worked loose during her training sessions. The training gym was empty and she was grateful it was just her and Jace. No witnesses for the lecture she was about to get.

Jace let her grab a drink before he started in. "You should've seen that coming." Yeah, she should've. Just like she should've predicted the last five hits he'd landed. "Keep your head in the fight, or the fight will take your head."

Maggie dropped her head back, rolled her neck. Dang, she was tired of that phrase.

"Cassie will talk with you...anytime."

Ugh, she was sick of that offer. She loved her new sister. Cassie was perfect for Jace and it was fun to watch her brother cater to the woman's every whim. Not that she had many. The girl was the most practical, down to earth being Maggie had ever met.

"Jace—"

"I know, Maggie, but you need to talk to *someone*. We can train you all we want but if you can't perform in the field..."

She lobbed towel at him. "I know, I know. I'm stuck working in the daycare."

It wasn't exactly punishment, but it'd feel like it despite the adorable kids. Mercury's children made up half the daycare and they were a delightful handful—a pudgy toddler and even chubbier babies. The experience would be pleasant enough, but Maggie's instincts weren't satisfied with herding children. The urge to hunt bad people, whatever the species, filled her.

Jace wiped his sweaty head down and tossed his towel in the laundry bin. "Meet you for target practice in the morning?"

"I'll be there."

He had taken it upon himself to conduct extra lessons outside of her normal training hours.

Her first week, she'd crawled back to her room in the lodge, spent from sessions getting worked over by the Guardians' resident trainer, Master Bellamy. Then the heartsick questions seized the opening, plaguing her, and she'd readily agreed to getting her butt handed to her by Jace day after day.

She waved to Jace as he left, wanting just a few moments to herself before she went to the locker room to clean up.

Why didn't Porter ever try to contact her?

What was he doing?

Had he moved on?

How could he move on after what they'd shared?

That bastard—

Ack! She clutched her head. The same questions and never any answers. Porter let her go, didn't come after her. He didn't call, didn't try to contact her in any way. He'd marked her! And thanks to Master Bellamy's lessons, she knew what the hell that meant. Heading into her second month without him, she didn't know how it would get any better.

Her broken heart remained a large, gaping mess, affecting her work, her training... Some days, she found herself alone at the table after a meal, having spaced out. Twice the showers ran cold on her because she may or may not have broken down sobbing in the shower.

Maggie jerked her head up. Someone was coming. Grabbing her water bottle and tossing her towel in the basket, she turned to leave only to meet Kaitlyn storming in, grumbling under her breath.

"Motherfucking cocksucker. Arrogant fucking prick. I want to snap his dick off."

Kaitlyn pulled up short when she noticed Maggie. "Oh, hey."

"Chayton?"

The redhead's face clouded over. "I came to pretend the punching bag is his ass." She assessed Maggie, likely reading the loneliness and despair she felt on a daily basis. "Want to pretend I'm an idiot mate with his head shoved up his ass, and I'll pretend you're a jerkoff with an inflated ego?"

Maggie grinned for the first time in a month. "Sounds divine."

***

Two more weeks…

Porter's hammer slipped, hitting the two-by-six. Metal clanged on the cement floor as the nail he'd been aiming for skidded across the room.

With a heavy sigh, he found the nail, bent at an atrocious angle.

Damn.

He flung it onto the pile he'd started of mangled nails—from just today.

It was no use. Porter gave up on his weekend of remodeling of the library's basement. Three of the walls had been erected yesterday. It had felt good to perform hard labor after sitting so many hours poring over old laws and policies

Seamus had either ignored or developed to suit his own needs.

Being the new mayor of Lobo Springs sucked ass some days.

Most days, he actually enjoyed it. Residents were coming out of their shells, optimism ran high despite the fact that Seamus was still at large. They were making headway, developing new procedures for peak function of the colony.

Trudging up the stairs, he wandered through the quiet library, marveling how its silence rivaled his home.

That sucked balls, too.

Outside, he was greeted by his beat up truck. It had been sitting right where he left it in the cheap motel's lot, looking like no one would want to steal it. Luckily, no one realized his toolbox held tools worth way more than his beater.

He was locking up when another pickup pulled up next to his.

"Denlan," Sanders greeted. "I saw you were here. Was checking to see if I could lend a hand."

Porter rubbed the back of his neck. "You always seem to know when I've put all my tools away." Actually, he was glad Sanders had missed him. He hadn't been good company for anyone lately. "I called it a day. I have some projects at home to get to. Did you get the bookshelves and end tables I dropped off with Betha?"

"Uh, yeah." Sanders shoved his hands into his jeans. "About that…We have more product than we can move in a month. Can you find another retailer to sell to?"

"What do you mean? Before I couldn't supply furniture fast enough."

Sanders tried really hard to keep pity out of his expression, but Porter smelled it. "That was before you spent every waking minute building, carving, staining..." He struggled, looking down at the pavement. "Have you talked to her at all?"

"She won't want to talk to me." There. Porter said the words that kept him up at night. His behavior drove her out of his house, and his life. His insomnia wasn't because he was sleeping on the living room floor. Her scent stayed preserved in his bedroom like a mausoleum of gigantic regrets.

"And you know that how?"

He was an asshole? He was selfish? Hadn't treated her wishes with respect? "Because I don't want to talk to me either." There it was. The flicker of sympathy in Sanders' eyes that reflected how pathetic Porter felt. "Besides, it'd do no good. Her life is there, mine is here." Porter stomped to his pickup to climb in and go back to his garage of solitude.

Was it sad that he'd moved everything out of his living room? Just being in his house was torture so he spent as little time within its walls as possible.

"Denlan, it's not the middle ages. It's not the days before cars were invented. We have these things now called phones, internet...Skype."

"Don't be a dick."

"I'm not, dude. Now that you're in charge, we have more internet access than ever."

Porter shook his head, resigned to the fact that Maggie was out of his life and it was because of him.

His friend refused to give up. "Meeting our mates doesn't mean everything's hunky-dory and we can live happily ever after. It means I'd better put the damn dishes away or Betha will stomp around the house mentioning everything else I don't listen to her about. It means that when she announced she wants to become an accountant, I'd better find some fake documents to help her go to school. It means that I have to apologize. A lot. Because she's never wrong."

Porter smiled despite himself. He adored Sanders and Betha. Not just because his friend had ripped the band aid off and revealed that yes, he thought the fairy tale came with the mating bond.

His smile faded. "I messed up, Sanders. Bad."

"We all do." Sanders clapped him on the back. "Get used to crawling back to her on your knees. It won't be the first time."

Porter considered Sanders' advice the entire ride home. What if he called Maggie and she told him to fuck off?

What if she didn't?

He hung onto that thought. For the first time in so many, many weeks hope bloomed. After all, it was either Maggie or no one. He couldn't imagine dredging up interest in another female any time in the next century.

That gave him years to grovel his way back into her heart.

So… How should he reach her? Drive within range and tap in telepathically? No, what if she was doing something important, like…fighting someone?

Email? No, he didn't know her address, or if she had one.

Phone? He didn't know her number.

Quit being a damn pussy and call the girl.

Every clan leader had a way to reach the Guardians. As the newly appointed mayor, the information was already in his computer. He just needed to dig in and find it. The contact wouldn't get him directly to Maggie, but close enough. Several of the Guardians were mated males. They'd know all about spontaneous idiotic episodes of male brain.

***

"Pass the peas, please." Armana smiled at Cassie.

Jace's mate grinned and passed the bowl of veggies Maggie had never seen her mom eat, proving she was really trying to gain ground with Jace. He was still cool toward her, but they continued their weekly dinners together in Jace's cabin, away from the others at the lodge.

Same dinner, different week. Maggie and Jace talked shop. Cassie chatted with Armana.

Maggie shoved the last mouthful of briquette in and chewed quickly. Jace had a plateful left because she'd asked him to explain how he invested the Guardians' holdings. While her financially minded brother geeked out, she finished dinner.

He wrapped up an explanation she only half followed. She pushed away from the table. "I'll get dishes tonight."

Cassie's shrewd mind interpreted what Maggie was doing. She snapped her fingers. "Shoot. I forgot I told Kaitlyn I'd stop by tonight." She smiled at Maggie and Armana, kissed her scowling mate and started for the door. "If you'll excuse me."

Silence filled the cabin once the door shut.

"Your mate doesn't lie very well, Jace." Armana smiled fondly.

Maggie chuckled, *almost* breaking Jace's sour mood, but he remained stout. "Cassie hasn't needed to lie to me." The tone of his statement sounded as if it ended with an unspoken *until you got here* aimed at their mother.

Armana's face fell, her hands folded on the table.

"It was my fault," Maggie interjected. "I wanted to change it up tonight so you two had a chance to talk. To each other."

"We've talked," Jace grumbled.

"I explained everything to you." Armana was folding her cloth napkin into tiny squares, then undoing it all to start over again. "But we haven't *talked* since then. I understand your feelings toward me, son. I wouldn't push it, I knew you needed time, but it appears to bother both your sister and your mate."

He threw his hands up, biceps bunching under his shirt's material. "What am I supposed to do? Say it's great talking to you after the last thirteen years of you cutting me out of your life?"

Her brother needed to back the hell off. "Jace—"

Armana held up a hand. "It's all right, Maggie. I can take a lot. You and Jace are alive and well. It's all I've wanted from the beginning, even after I lost your father and Keve." Armana's voice broke on the last few words.

Maggie and Jace glanced at each other.

"I'm sorry, Ma." Maggie sat back in her chair to hug her mom. "I've never thought of how awful it was for you."

Jace slouched back in his chair, too. "Look, it's not that I don't want in you back in my life." He shrugged. "Before I left home, it was a push-pull between us. We argued half the time, then…nothing. I don't know to act around you now. It's like we're strangers."

"He's right, Ma." Maggie caught her mom's gaze. "It's like you're still you, but we're different."

Armana grabbed Maggie's hand, reaching out for Jace, whose brows drew down like he wondered if his mom really wanted them to chain together holding hands. She beckoned him with her fingers. He finally rested his palm on hers, easily dwarfing it.

"We start from here." Armana squeezed them both. "We have each other, and we have Cassie and the Guardians." She turned to Maggie, her nurturing mom expression in full force. "And it'll work out for you and Porter. Like us, he has things to work out."

Maggie tried to prevent doubt and loneliness from registering on her face, but Jace picked up on it. "You really want him back?"

Sighing, she freed her hand from her mom and crossed her arms, suddenly defensive. "Come on. Has it always been smooth sailing between you and Cassie?"

"No. She stabbed me in the back. Literally."

Armana's mouth dropped open with Maggie's.

He nodded to say *yeah, totally*. "I'll tell you the story sometime. She did it to save us. Totally different reason than Denlan."

"That may be so, but we live a long time, with passionate emotions—including anger." Armana's gaze turned retrospective. "Bane could piss me off like no one else."

"Dad?" Maggie's few memories were of gentle words and a big laugh.

"Oh, darling. One day, after I spent the whole night up with you when you were a baby, he took Keve to run in the woods. It had stormed the night before and he didn't think anything of it. Thought there was no issue with letting Keve run home—and through the house—on all four muddy paws."

"I remember that," Jace chimed in, focusing on the table like he was prying the episode out of a locked vault. "You handed a squalling Maggie to Dad and left. You were gone for the rest of the day and all night."

Armana's blue eyes crinkled at the corners. "I ran the woods and remained a wolf to sleep in the woods all night."

"And you came back to a spotless house," Jace finished.

They all laughed. Maggie was struck with how good this felt, for the first time in months, she felt like things might turn out all right.

Then the chasm Porter left in her life yawned wide.

"Have you dreamed anything?" Armana asked.

Maggie shook her head. "I've tried. Nothing on Porter." *Nothing.* "I think I pick up Seamus once in a while, but it's like incoherent fury. I sense his complete identity is wrapped up in Lobo Springs. In his mind, he made the town and it turned on him and he can't focus his rage."

Jace drummed his fingers. "Have you told the commander?"

"It only happened twice, and I couldn't determine where he was other than in the wild. But yes, I reported it both times."

"Good."

The three went quiet again until Armana broke the silence. "I'd love to hear about what you both do during the day."

Maggie was relieved she wouldn't have to go back to her room and be alone with her thoughts of how shitty her life was without Porter. She and Jace talked over each other, entertaining their mom well into the night.

Chapter Thirteen

Maggie was getting worse, not better. Huffing up a steep incline, she clawed with her hands to the crest and jumped as far as she could to the other side. Branches scraped her face, dirt and debris clung to her skin, but still she ran.

If Jace saw her, he'd say she should be in her wolf form. If Master Bellamy knew what she was up to, he'd say she needed to run smarter. The mad speed she tore through the woods with wasn't about training or adapting to her heritage. It was about running until she couldn't feel the loss and betrayal that laced every thought of Porter Denlan. Running until she numbed to the pain throbbing in her heart.

Her pace increased. She passed the boundaries of the Guardians' wards, uncaring of the repercussions. She was sick of being confined, tired of every one using their heartbreak home brews on her. Escape was a necessity for her sanity.

The visit with her mother and Jace two nights ago had turned out well. She'd went to bed so optimistic only to lie awake all night and drag ass the next morning.

Circumventing tree trunks, low hanging branches, and thick underbrush, her sneakers took the abuse. By the time she was done, they'd be shredded. Maybe they'd let her out to go to town and shop.

Yes! Maybe that was it. She just needed to get out. She woke up to lessons with Jace, spent the day getting kicked around by a centuries-old shifter who didn't look much older than her mother, went to bed getting her ass handed to her by Kaitlyn. In between, when she tried to eat, Cassie showed up to "talk."

Actually, her sister really was just trying to get to know her, but Maggie wasn't in a place to chat. Because she didn't want to just pick Cassie's therapist brain, she wanted her to be a crystal ball and tell her whether Porter was done with her.

It should be Maggie who was done with him. Pining for a male she'd known less than a week—ridiculous. Jace tried convincing her it was the mating bond. If only! Her mother was steadfast that all would be all right, Maggie just needed to relax and let it happen.

Relax? Her hormones kept her up at night, writhing in bed because her body yearned for his touch, and stealing her focus during the day. She held on to every detail of their late night cuddle talking about their lost loved ones, how he snatched her out of Seamus' way when he vaulted out of the window, then buffered her fall with himself, and that last night together when they really connected.

~203~

One day, she'd watched Kaitlyn nibble on chocolate. The deep brown squares reminded her of the color of Porter's eyes. *Pathetic!* And she knew it but couldn't help the feelings tormenting her.

Cars humming in the distance alerted Maggie that she was getting closer to the highway. Even though she was running as a human, she craved complete isolation. Adjusting her course, she charged deeper into the trees.

The only saving grace to the last two months was that no one told her to move on, encouraging her to head to Pale Moonlight, meet some male shifters, and purge Porter from her system. This mate business was serious shit, and apparently she wandered unchartered territory getting rejected by hers.

Alas, despite how her heart yearned for its mate, he ranked as a complete asshat and Maggie needed to discover a way to live without him and reach her full potential.

But what if he came groveling back…No! The gut wrenching feelings on the what-if cruise were dangerous.

He'd had two months. If he crawled on his knees back to her, he'd have reached her by now.

Slowing to a stop, she rested her hands on her hips until she caught her breath. Scanning the woods, she discerned how far out she was. Time to get back.

Pivoting, she loped along the same path she'd plowed on her way out.

An awareness dawned on her, beginning with a tingle along her spine, like she was being watched.

Pretending nothing was amiss, with each inhale she breathed deeply. The scent of another shifter tinted the air. A male.

The Guardians mentioned other shifters ran the area outside of West Creek. Heavily wooded with few recreation areas for humans, it was the safest place to run their wolves for miles.

She tasted the air again. This scent was familiar. Where had she encountered it before? It was like…tobacco?

A loud pop preceded heat searing through her leg. She lost her balance, careening into the ground, rolling until she clotheslined a tree trunk. The breath *whooshed* from her lungs.

The male approached, she rolled to her good side, trying to regain her bearings.

Get up! Assess the situation.

The first observation was that she'd been shot. The second item in her assessment was her lack of a weapon. Rookie mistake. The others never went anywhere without a weapon strapped to them, unless they were furry with four legs.

Hand-to-hand combat it was. Rising to her good leg, she dropped to a fighting crouch. A chuckle from the right had her hopping around to see the shifter. Her injured leg screamed with the movement, the scent of her blood permeated the air.

Seamus.

He stalked toward her, his menacing presence clogging the air around them. His thick-bodied swagger ate up the space between them. Mean intelligence shone in his eyes and Maggie realized how much she'd discredited his threat to Lobo Springs, to her. Wearing grass-stained slacks and a ripped silk shirt, the male could've strolled into a board room and commanded every ounce of attention.

His green eyes glowed, he was the predator and she the prey. A smug grin twisted his mouth. "I knew it was only a matter of time before they let you out. The Guardians have quit searching for me, thinking I slunk into the hills to lick my wounds. I don't give up what's mine." He raised a sinister black gun, aiming it point blank at her head.

Ohshitohshitohshit.

She darted to the left, diving and rolling so her good leg took the brunt of the fall. Seamus tackled her, rolling her onto her back. She landed only a few punches; he straddled her, mercilessly grinding down on her injury with his knee.

Stars filled her vision, her teeth ground into each other to keep from screaming—out loud. Instead, she broadcasted to every Guardian who popped into her mind.

Seamus is here and he's got me!

"The only way to get back what's mine is to take what's his." He sneered, pressing the cool barrel of the gun to her temple.

Porter—

Her blackout immediately followed the blast.

***

Porter sat on the floor, a.k.a. his bed for the last two months. The number to the West Creek Guardians scrawled on the yellow sticky note he held between his fingers. He thought of circling his bedroom again, to torture himself with how much he missed her, how vitally important it was he attempt to get her back and then keep at it until she relented.

What if she didn't forgive him? Could he blame her? After Sanders helped him see the light, the town had suddenly needed him every waking minute. He'd come home, convincing himself to call only to realize how late it was and then justify how he couldn't disturb the Guardians at that hour. If only the number he had was a direct line to Maggie. That was his biggest concern. He'd call; they'd hang up. Finally, he had a reprieve and there was no way to find out if he didn't make the damn call.

His heart jackhammering in his chest, he pulled out his phone.

Porter!

Jerking back, his phone clattered to the floor, the note fluttered away, but he ignored it.

Maggie?

Silence.

Maggie?

Nothing.

Maggie!

He searched for the phone. Nimbly picking it up, he dialed, the number branded into mind.

She'd sounded like she was in pain, that one word steeped in panic.

The phone rang and rang.

Porter hit end and resend. More ringing, still no answer.

End. Resend.

Ring.

No answer.

End. Resend.

"Motherfucker, Denlan!" Jace's exasperated voice finally answered. "What!"

"Where is she?"

"What do you care?"

"Where. Is. She."

Jace exhaled a long suffering breath. "Gone. She got out a message that Seamus found her. We're scouring the area."

What was she doing out of the wards with Seamus loose? If he asked, Jace would likely hang up and he *needed* information on Maggie. "Where was she taken?"

"We'll find her. Go back to being a mayor, Denlan." Jace disconnected.

Asshole!

Porter dialed another number. Voice mail picked up. "Sanders. Maggie's in trouble, I need to go. You need to take over for me."

Rushing around his house, he gathered anything he might need in as little time as possible. Seamus wasn't going to flee with Maggie into city limits. He'd be a fish out of water, only he wouldn't have the decency to suffocate and die. Porter was heading toward the garage when he stopped and turned back.

Throwing open his closet door, he rummaged around until he found the small rectangular box from his father. The gleaming silver Ruger he and his father used for target practice lay inside. He counted the rounds.

Enough to fill the cylinder and take Seamus down to get his head ripped off.

Chapter Fourteen

Maggie's head pounded. The slight rocking motion encouraged the throbbing.

Suppressing a groan, she maintained awareness without opening her eyes. *Remember, remember.*

Seamus. Shot in the leg. Shot in the head.

He was using her to get back at Porter.

Not a surprise.

Situational awareness: Seamus was pissed, possibly feral, and gunning for revenge. But…his disadvantages included being a shifter fugitive and perhaps—hopefully—not knowing she was training to become a Guardian.

Location: The rocking motion and engine purr suggested Seamus was driving her somewhere. The rush of wind from a cracked window filtered out only some of the cigarette smoke clogging the air.

Working from head to toe, she performed a self-systems check. Clothing still on, thank the Sweet Mother. She smelled dried blood on her running leggings and shirt. Her leg should be healed, her head well on its way. Yet her leg ached as severely as her noggin. The bullets. They were still in her.

She tried to call out to Jace mentally. Her stomach twisted, she barely held back a heave.

That complicated things. She'd have to factor tenacious pain into her plans. Her wrists were bound behind her back and her ankles were cuffed. A sick notion occurred to her and she really hoped Seamus didn't use his BDSM restraints. Because that would be gross.

Funny how the most ridiculous worries came to mind when she had more dire issues occurring.

"I can tell you're awake." Seamus' deep rumble reached her ears.

Damn.

"I can finally see again after you shot me in the head," she bit back.

"You called out, I had to shut you up." He spoke so frankly. No big deal to him that he plugged a bullet into her brain. Business as usual.

Recovering from severe injury was new to her, expected at some point, but she supposed the first time was always a shock. Absolutely would've preferred complete mending. A hunk of lead still lodged in her brain—and her leg—sapped her strength, and he knew it.

Opening her eyes, the stark interior of a van sent chills crawling up her spine. If this was the same van what's-his-name kicked it in, she'd vomit. She might vomit anyway.

Guardians do not puke from fear! Act like one, think like one. "So what's your plan? Are you going to spill all the diabolical details, or leave me guessing?"

He flicked the remains of his smoke out the window and closed it. "Well," increasing her dread, the van turned off onto a rougher road, taking her farther away from any civilization, "Denlan took everything from me. I can't kill him and take it back because the Guardians are involved. But I heard the talk about you and him while I was in hiding. So I'll take you from him."

Maggie interpreted that to mean traitors lived in Lobo Springs and were actively plotting against Porter.

Her pounding brain said she shouldn't care. Porter's a big boy, he can take care of himself. Her tender heart remembered who she called out to before she was knocked out. Silly girl. Mental communication over hundreds of miles wasn't possible, yet she'd wasted the chance to pass more information, instead calling out to the male she loved.

No wonder she was failing Guardian training despite being born to do it. She was as hopelessly naïve in her love life as well as shifter life.

"How's it going to go down?" she asked. "You drop my body on his doorstep? Scavenger hunt to find my remains? Dismember and scatter?"

His deep chuckle bounced off the walls of the work van. "Good ideas, Mage. I haven't decided yet. I know I want him to suffer not knowing where you are. Word is he's been a shell of himself, nothing but work to fill his days since you decided Lobo Springs wasn't good enough for a city girl."

She'd be lying if she said that didn't make her deliriously happy. One, because he should suffer, too. Two, because his feeling of loss matched hers and he wasn't dealing either.

"I want him to suffer," Seamus voice dropped a menacing octave, "wondering what I'll be doing to you."

What a coincidence. That was the nagging unease eating at Maggie's gut. She was a female captured by a notoriously deprived male.

"That would be what?" Better to know what to prepare for, but she hoped he didn't answer.

"Use your imagination."

***

Porter sped down the highway. He'd already been pulled over once. Waiting for the cop to saunter to the window, stroll back to his patrol car with Porter's documents, run his information, then write up a ticket, and finally let him go had tested every ounce of patience Porter possessed.

Pushing the speed at ten over, he kept a keen eye out for any more law enforcement. The windows were rolled down so any hint of Maggie's divine scent—or Seamus' atrocious one—would blow through the cab.

Leaving Lobo Springs, his internal debate between flying to Guardian headquarters in West Creek or scour the countryside had remained unresolved until he hit the highway. The Guardians would be—better fucking be—out looking for her. His arrival on their doorstep would do no good if they weren't there.

The other option of driving around the countryside sounded like a field exercise in futility, *if* it hadn't been for Porter's intuition screaming at him. He swung a hammer for a living—good honest work. Now he led Lobo Springs—an honorable position he took seriously. Being an evil dick who lived for terrorizing others wasn't on his resume.

Say it was... What would he do in Seamus' place?

While Porter had flown down the road, he put himself in Seamus' mind frame. Revenge, obviously. How had he known what Maggie meant to him?

Two months and Porter had sensed no disquiet. Because those who were Seamus supporters were helping him, patiently waiting for Porter's downfall.

He could be like a robot, just going through the motions of life, so long as she was safe and content four hours away. But he'd be worthless if he ever *lost* her. The sobering thought gave him insight to his dad's last decision to throw the fight with Seamus.

Porter would hand over Lobo Springs to have Maggie back in his arms.

To keep himself from tearing away while waiting for his speeding ticket, he'd calculated. To be in the general vicinity as Seamus, if the bastard was heading back home to finalize his retribution, Porter needed to drive another hour and a half.

Recalling what lay between Lobo Springs and Freemont, Porter formulated a plan of his own. Twin Lakes was a small town the highway cut through. The only reason it was still on the map was recreation. Its name originated from the two large lakes, one on each side of the highway, but several miles off on either side. During the year, no matter the season, Twin Lakes provided equipment for every activity and more importantly, reservations for the many cabins that surrounded each lake.

If he was a soulless shitbag, he'd take Maggie to a desolate cabin, defile her as much as possible before the Guardians could track his scent, and then taunt Porter with the location of any remains he decided to leave behind.

The speedometer needle crept up. Porter eased his foot off the gas. He had another hour before he reached Twin Lakes and he'd need one hell of a strategy.

Chapter Fifteen

Maggie didn't know any of the geography around Freemont. Her one trip to her hometown didn't help her much. The path Seamus took shook the van so badly she knew they weren't on the highway, hadn't been for a while.

Rolling forward on her shoulder as the van slowed, Maggie raised her head to attempt a glimpse out the window. They were stopping for good, or for supplies. She couldn't smell much within the van, the lead on her brain lessened her senses, but she sensed civilization, albeit at a lower level than a metropolis like Freemont.

Tires crunched, the van pulled to stop.

Seamus twisted in his seat, his cruel gaze narrowed on her. "If you make a sound, I'll choke you until you shut up. And I'll enjoy it."

"Noted."

He stepped from the vehicle and the familiar sounds of a cap unscrewing, metal thunking, and the rhythmic clicks of gas pumping permeated the walls of the vans.

If Seamus had been keeping low, then he'd be using cash to escape electronic tracking of a card. He'd have to pay inside.

She tested her bindings. They were solid, but she was a shifter. One of his followers must've smuggled Seamus' supplies to him—an old lover perhaps? He could've bought new restraints, but these reeked of rough sex, and he had needed to stay out of sight. A set circled her wrists and a similar pair secured her ankles. Tapping into everything she learned working at the store, she mentally logged their details, thinking like a Guardian. Extreme bondage cuffs, fur-lined leather, with a metal lock that hooked to a ring secured by a leather strap. Seamus must've gambled on being around to beat or shoot her if she got out of line. He didn't gamble on her being trained by the best for the last two months, or that she knew about these cuffs and where their weak points were. Thank The Gift Shop.

This was her only chance.

Closing her eyes, she visualized every muscle fiber contracting, pulling her wrists and legs in opposite directions. Leather snapped taut, pinching her skin.

But she felt give. With more force, she could tear the ring through the material. Stopping to make sure Seamus wasn't coming back into the van, she went lax.

Huffing out a breath, she willed her breathing to remain steady and she listened.

~217~

The rhythmic clicks stopped, the nozzle put back on its rest, the gas cap replaced. Steps retreated from the vehicle.

Eyes squeezed shut, she concentrated her efforts once again. Joints popped against the strain. Gritting her teeth, straining until every muscle bulged, every vein stood prominent, the leather frayed around the ring until it released her legs. The cuffs were still an issue. The angles of her arms made it difficult to create enough force.

Wiggling her aching arms past her butt and down her legs, she maneuvered them in front of her. Bracing herself against the pain, she wedged a foot between her wrists to add another source of pressure.

Finally, the ring holding the lock ripped through on one side. Maggie flew back, spread eagle, stunned it actually worked.

Victory celebration later.

She shot over the passenger seat, grabbed Seamus' matches, and unlocked the door. Rolling out and dropping in a crouch, she spared a glance around.

The rest stop was small, once she crossed the main road, three steps and she'd be in the safety of the trees. The slight breeze carried only human redolence. Even better.

From her position, she was blocked from the store by the van. She pulled her shirt off and punched buttons on the gas pump. She released the nozzle and soaked her shirt in gasoline to use as fuel for the diversion she planned. Securing the lever for continuous gas release, she dropped it on the ground a few feet in front of her. Then she kicked her shoes off, lit a match and used it to set aflame the rest of the matches in the book.

The slight tremor in her hand nearly extinguished the tiny fire. Carefully, she set the book on top of her shoes. With a hiss, the rest of the book caught fire and began to burn through the top of her shoe that rested on the soaked shirt. Her fear was that the soggy shirt would put out the flame before it caught fire or the vapors would catch too quickly and take her up with it. The time it took to set her diversion would cost precious minutes, but if it worked, she at least had a tiny chance in hell at escape.

Taking off at the fastest sprint she'd ever run, her leg screamed in pain. Her jostled brain exploded stars in her vision. Tendrils of awareness tickled her neck. Seamus saw her!

She made it across the street before she heard his shout. Digging deep, she excavated her well of speed.

An explosion shuddered the air around her. A bright blaze flashed in her periphery, followed by a heat wave that warmed her clammy skin.

Sparing a glance back, she almost stopped to jump up and down in delight. The nozzle she'd left lying next to her pile, acted like a wick for the flames to blow the pump which blew the van. Since

Seamus wasn't charging after her, he must've been on the other side.

The edge of the woods grew closer. She didn't care who saw, as soon as she broke into the trees, she shed her bra and leggings and unstrapped the remains of each cuff. Plowing as deep into the woods as she dared, she shifted.

The rush of power through her body as four legs hit the ground was addicting. The adrenaline pumping through her blood added to it. Maggie's senses were dulled, but the shift into her wolf helped define each scent. The most important one was that Seamus wasn't pursing her—yet.

She'd utilize every scrap of shifter and Guardian knowledge she'd obtained in the last two months to keep Seamus from finding her. It was time to live up to her destiny.

***

Porter parked at the first convenience store he encountered when he reached Twin Lakes. Stepping out of his truck, he lifted his nose. The faint smell of smoke in the air clogged his nose enough that he couldn't pick up finer detail, like whether Maggie had recently been through the area.

The wail of a siren assaulted his sensitive ears. Spinning around, he saw a fire truck turn off the highway onto a two lane road that disappeared into the countryside. It wasn't unusual to have fire emergencies in tourist areas, especially if they involved campfires. It was a warm late spring day, a camper might've been up late with roasting s'mores over a fire pit.

A second siren alerted him to another truck. He watched that vehicle head in the same direction. The flashing light disappeared yet Porter couldn't tear his eyes away.

His intuition prickled enough to prompt him to gather information on where the trucks were headed.

A buzzer sounded his entrance into the store. Cool air conditioning wafted over his heated skin. His distress over what Maggie might be experiencing stoked his core temp until he worried he'd steam in the A/C.

He grabbed the first thing in arm's reach. At the counter, he was thrilled to see a man well past middle age. The older humans always knew what was going on around them and wanted to talk about everything, especially in a small town.

Plopping his—Porter frowned—bulbous pink lollipop on the counter, he faced the cashier, who eventually tore his gaze from the window.

"A fire bad enough for two engines, huh?" Porter kept his tone light, curious.

"Oh yeah." The guy leaned over the counter, speaking low even though Porter was certain he'd tell his gossip to everyone who entered. "My scanner said there was an explosion at Stop 'n' Supply." He pulled back. "Shame, too, because it's the only stop for gas and essentials before you reach the campgrounds."

"Accidental?"

The guy scanned the empty store before answering. "The 9-1-1 caller said he saw a woman start a fire by the pump."

Blood drained from Porter's face, taking all his excess heat along with it. "Did she escape?"

His salt-and-pepper head bobbed. "Said she took off and kept going."

Porter vacillated between slamming his fist into the counter and grabbing the dude to hug him. "Anyone hurt?"

"The witness said a man was caught in the explosion." He shook his head mournfully. "I hope he's okay and that everyone made it out of the store."

Porter hoped everyone inside the store was fine, too. The guy caught in the flames could fucking fry if it was Seamus.

It also meant Seamus had only held her for a few hours and most of it had been driving.

"Thanks, man." Porter threw a five on the counter, grabbed the sucker so the human wouldn't run after him thinking he forgot it, and rushed back to his truck.

He avoided burning rubber across the highway in his hurry to get to the site of the explosion. Law enforcement would definitely be arriving in the area. He set the cruise control so his nerves wouldn't cause him to stomp down on the gas pedal.

Holding the wheel with one hand, he thumbed through his phone to pull up a map of the area. The screen went black and the cursor kept circling 'round.

"Fuck!" He tossed it onto his seat so he wouldn't crush the useless piece of high-tech. If Twin Lakes had shit service, no way was he going to get a signal driving farther away from it.

Gentle curves meandered through the wooded area surrounding the lake. Nothing Porter needed full concentration for to navigate.

He focused so he wouldn't broadcast to any shifters in the vicinity. *Maggie?*

Grinding his teeth, knuckles white on the steering wheel, he waited.

Nothing.

Maggie!

Three possibilities came to mind. She wasn't in the area, she was ignoring him, or she was too injured to respond. Any one of them was entirely possible.

He picked up his phone again. No signal was in the cards today.

Throwing his hand over the wheel, he leaned out his open window enough to receive the full blast of air. The stench of smoke grew stronger. He had no idea how Maggie's scent could cut through it, or if he was even on the right road.

Finally, he spotted a sign for Stop 'n' Supply. Ten more miles.

A highway patrol car approached from behind and sped around him. Another good sign he was heading to the right place.

Slowing as he neared, he drew back inside so as to not attract attention hanging his head out the window.

A patrolmen stood a block away from a cluster of fire trucks, ambulances, and police cars—every EMS vehicle the county possessed. He waved Porter to the farthest edge of the road and held out a hand to stop him.

Porter pulled up. The officer pointed him down a side road. "You can't go through the rest area. You can reach the campground from here, but if you need supplies you'll have to go back to Twin Lakes."

"No problem." Porter glanced at the conglomeration, noting a blackened van much like the ones Seamus favored. "Thank you, sir."

Ambling down the stretch of road, Porter envisioned his beautiful mate and tried again. *Maggie?*

Silence.

After a few miles, the sign for the campground appeared. Porter pulled into the main lot by the information shack. Only two other cars sat in the lot. They belonged to humans either deeper on the grounds camping or out for a hike.

Porter took his shirt off after he got out of the truck and set it on the seat. Eyeing the box containing the Ruger, he untied his work boots and slipped them off. Setting the boots on the floor, he reached to flip the box open. Extracting the revolver and ammo, he loaded all six slots in the cylinder. Rolling his flannel up tightly, he tied off the end, then looped the arms around to tie off a loop.

Next he shrugged out of his t-shirt and locked his pickup. The keys he hid back behind a tire. Tucking the flannel and its cargo under his arm, he loped off into the trees.

The tang of smoke clung to him, but he couldn't scent any humans around. Setting his bundle down, he stripped out of his pants and shifted.

His senses came alive. Raising his head to sniff the air he promptly sneezed. The acrid tang of burning gasoline dulled his acute sense of smell. He'd have to cast a wide net searching for a sign Maggie or Seamus was in the area.

Nosing through his shirt wrap, he ducked his head into the loop and wiggled it down his neck. The wolf side of him frowned on the collar-like contraption, but he didn't know what arsenal Seamus had with him. Porter wanted every advantage searching for Maggie—and for when he found Seamus.

Chapter Sixteen

Maggie's leg burned. Fantasies of getting her hands on a blade and digging the lead out fueled her flee. Running as fast as her limp allowed, she navigated trees, avoided jumping over any downed trunks to keep her head from pounding until her eyes crossed, and set a course for the lake.

The fish-laced odor of lake water grew stronger. She focused on it to crowd out the smell of the fire. With each passing mile, the smoke lessened as the wind helped carry it into the atmosphere.

The throbbing in her skull urged her to slow down, keep her heartbeat from creating the cacophony behind her eyes. She couldn't; decreasing her speed meant opening a window of opportunity for Seamus. She was naïve about her world, but not enough to think the explosion had decimated him, or even better, blew his cruel face off. The van took the brunt of it, and Seamus was devious enough to escape the humans' concern over his injuries, or his resurrection from sure death.

Vegetation thinned and blue twinkled through the branches. The sight allowed Maggie to slow. She sniffed the ground searching for recent human presence. Nothing. Using narrow tree trunks for cover, she inspected her surroundings.

This portion of Twin Lakes was a sizable body of water. Cabins dotted the shoreline. Some of the more affluent buildings had personal docks, but to Maggie's good fortune, the public dock and beach were on the other side of the lake. Since it was a weekday and not peak season, lake activity was pretty quiet. Only a few boats dotted the water.

She'd have to chance the notice of the fishermen. With her speed hindered, her aching brain would have to come up with various ways to hide from Seamus.

Trotting to the edge of the water, she sniffed around to make sure she was alone. Edging closer, the squishy coolness of mud caked her paws. She didn't sink as much as she would've on two legs, but as a shifter-sized wolf, her paws settled in.

Dammit. That left prints. If Seamus' sense of smell recovered quickly from its combustive assault, he'd have no problem following her. She wasn't as concerned about that as she was about leaving massive paw prints for humans to find. Her Guardian training to conceal their existence kicked in. The fishers might think she was a larger than average wolf from their distance away, but she didn't have to give them proof.

Shuffling her feet through the thick muck, she obscured as much as she could before stepping into the water. Cold shocked her legs, traveling up her spine until she shivered and jerked her tail. Treading in deeper, her feet sinking even farther in the mud, wisps of green algae clinging to her fur, she stalled to let her body adjust to the temperature.

The pounding in her temples slowed, the ache in her leg dimmed, the cold's soothing properties working on her injuries. If only she could hang out in the water until a shifter besides Seamus found her.

With the bullet's effects diminished, she considered attempting telepathy again. Focusing on the surface of the water, the swish of each lap of wave hitting land, the feel of green algae swirling around her legs, she tried reaching out to her brother.

Ja—

She jerked her head as if to yank it away from the source of pain, the sounds of the water diminished, threatening her consciousness. Her face hit the water, effectively waking her up when she would've passed out.

No telepathy. She doubted she'd be able to receive any mental communications and she sincerely hoped that if anyone tried, she wouldn't writhe in agony from the pain or that it wouldn't instantly knock her out.

Moving to deeper water for the camouflage and so she wouldn't expend so much energy schlepping through the mud, she counted on instincts taking over. As a person, she'd never went swimming. Her assumption that her wolfy self would know how to doggy paddle had better hold true or she was screwed. To her right was more open shoreline. Several hundred yards away was a cabin nestled in the trees. Her chance of concealment lay to her left where the ground swelled. The water had cut through the face of the hill until it rose over the water twenty-feet. Maggie planned to swim around that until she reached an area she could exit the water from.

Seamus could follow her scent *to* the water, but not *through* the water.

Jerky movements subsided and her instincts took over. She stuck close to shore in case she ran into trouble swimming and concentrated on maintaining calm breathing. Flatter shore dissolved into an incline that held no purchase for a creature with no hands. The depth of water increased, the temperature of the water dropping with it. Rolling waves splashed her face, but she powered through. Fatigue set in. If the full body cold compress hadn't soothed her aches, she wouldn't have made the trip.

She still wasn't sure she would. The sheer surface on her left kept curving, continuing for how long she didn't know.

Dull pounding built between her ears. A constant crescendo would develop if she didn't get rest. And even then, she didn't know if it'd go away.

Her sides heaved, the effort getting to be too much.

There was no one else out here to help her. Sure, the Guardians, or at least Jace and her mother would come looking for her. Finding her would be akin to the needle in a haystack. Once Seamus had dumped her body in the van and drove off, her scent had left with it. No way in hell would they have tracked her to this lake out in the middle of nowhere. Even if they surmised Seamus would bring her to Lobo Springs for his retribution, they wouldn't have enough manpower to scour the miles of territory around the village.

She was alone.

Porter's handsome face, his steady, dark gaze and strong body, came to mind.

If she could spare the air, she'd sigh. Before she was shot, he was her last thought. Facing her possible end in murky, frigid water, he was last on her mind.

He'd hurt her, but it wasn't anything that couldn't be repaired. Sheer stubbornness and dented feelings had kept them apart. Here she was, ready to tell him she loved his headstrong hide. They could find a way to make their long distance relationship work. They had centuries!

Had centuries. Maggie might only have minutes. Hours, if she was lucky. Days, if there was a miracle in store for her.

The slap of waves against the earth changed to the gentle splash of waves carrying through vegetation.

Thank the Sweet Mother. In a hundred yards, the land sloped back down. The rugged shoreline gradually formed from cattails and reeds. It'd be perfect concealment. Another hundred yards was a cabin. No boats sat at the short dock, she sensed no cars or people. It warranted a closer look.

Using the tall grasses and plants for cover, she trudged out of the water. Her legs wobbled, she panted, her tongue lolling out. Damn, she was tired. Unconsciousness did not equate sleep and it'd been a long day, her injuries dragging her further down.

Shivers grew into full body shakes. Cold, tired, and injured weren't a winning combination. Circling the cabin in her halting, plodding stride, she determined that it was empty.

No cars were visible in the front. The flower beds hadn't been worked up yet after winter, leaves and debris scattered in front of the door.

It was worth a shot.

She glanced around, the openness around the cabin made her feel like a large, red target had been painted on her flanks. It had to be done. She'd bought herself some time, now she needed to take care of herself.

Rising to her hind legs, she fell back to all fours with a whimper. The bullet. Shifting her stance, taking the brunt of her weight on her good leg, she tested the knob. Her wet, muddy paws slipped and slid.

This wouldn't work. Searching the trees one last time, she flowed back into her human form.

Sagging against the door, her raging headache and burning leg sapped her energy. Cold dimpled her body from head to toe. Teeth chattering, she wondered if shifters could die of hypothermia or if they just laid dormant until warmer weather arrived.

She tested the door again. Locked of course. Using the walls for support, she tested all the windows and back door, hoping none of the boaters could see a naked woman trying to break into one of the cabins. If she was reported and the police came, she'd feed them some stereotypical story about an abusive husband chasing her—a gamble that they don't watch the same shows she did.

To prevent the possibility, she stumbled back to the front door. It had the most secure lock, but the stoop was more private. When she reached it, she leaned against the door to catch her breath. Jiggling the handle, the lock seemed sturdy.

Shoving her body against it would take too much effort. She needed to make sure her assault on the door counted. Taking three steps back, she prepped herself.

One, two, three…

Using her good leg as the foundation, she focused on the area above the handle and stomped her bad leg into the door.

Her thigh screamed as her foot slammed through the door. The door jumped and groaned, but remained solid. Ignoring the pain, digging deep, she kicked again, and again, the bullet wedged in her flexing muscles tearing healed flesh apart.

Finally, the door shuttered open and Maggie fell through, landing on the chilly hardwood floor. She rolled on her butt and measured her surroundings. No cameras were visible; no wires ran from the door. There was no keypad and so she hoped, no security system. It was plain inside—walls, a living area and kitchenette under an arched ceiling, and a small room off to the side.

The one level dwelling made it easier with her limited mobility to locate a bedroom with possible clothing. The dresser in the room was empty, the bed stripped down to the mattress, leaving Maggie's only hope the closet.

Come on, even a towel.

With hands shaking from the chill, she pulled open the closet door.

Empty.

Refusing to cry from frustration, she spun around. She had to pick the cabin with the most thorough tenants ever, who scoured everything before they left for the winter.

Limping to the door, a piece of fabric under the bed caught her eye. She snagged it. It was a dusty old t-shirt. One someone had used as a rag. To Maggie it was like a cashmere sweater. She shook it out and pulled it on. It was long enough to cover her butt cheeks, but as tight as a sausage casing.

Heading for the kitchen, she wondered if her luck would hold.

Empty. All but two jars of home canned green beans and from the looks of the contents, Maggie didn't feel like testing whether shifters could survive botulism.

The sight of swampy green beans rumbled her belly.

She muttered to herself. "No luck, hunger. You and I are going to be pals."

She tested the sink but the water had been shut off. She'd gotten enough mouthfuls swimming to keep her going. If she had more energy, she'd get it working to shower, but rest took priority. That, and getting the bullet out of her leg. She found a knife, long and sharp and set it on the counter, but she didn't know if she could dig out the bullet in her thigh without bleeding out or staying conscious. If both scenarios occurred, she'd be screwed. With no food, she couldn't heal.

She needed sleep before she could do anything.

The couch in the small living room promised more warmth than the plastic covered mattress. Maggie hobbled over, her vision beginning to blur from her migraine. Rest, then change into a wolf and hope to catch something with a little meat on its bones during her flee.

Closing her eyes, she sought relief, but none came. Only exhaustion overwhelmed her pain so she could fall asleep.

In her slumber she saw a chocolate brown wolf with a red handkerchief tied around his neck.

Porter?

He ran through the trees at a pace faster than she'd ever dare, his face set, determined. The fabric around his neck bounced rhythmically like it contained a small but weighty load. She recognized the fallen tree he'd just passed. Had he found her trail?

The lake came into view and he charged to the water. Stopping, he sniffed around, his tail taut and pointed. Lifting his head, he searched the midnight water, moonlight twinkling over the waves. Tasting the air, he looked left, then right. He continued to do that as if dumbfounded.

His thoughts ran through her head. *She's smart, what would she do in this situation? She's running from Seamus, needs to lose her scent.* He eyed toward the right, noting the increase in human activity like she had. Knew that heading that direction meant Seamus would pick up her trail easier, maybe even intersect her.

The other direction was the only answer. *She wouldn't have backtracked because the risk of running into Seamus was too high.*

Porter sped toward the right. Maggie was confused. He spun and ran into the trees and right back out, leaping into the water with a splash.

Had he done it to confuse the trail? His jump from several feet away would keep his scent from trailing into the water.

Her mate swam much better than she had, but then he'd been doing it his whole life. Like hers, his mind wandered during the swim, his thoughts settling on her.

His emotions filtered through. Terror for her safety. It was greater than her own fear for her life. Regret. So much regret, of what he'd said, of their time apart, of how he should've come begging her forgiveness so at least she'd know he loved her.

Maggie shifted on the couch, a sob escaping.

No! She didn't want to quit dreaming. If she woke up and it was all just a fantasy, she'd be devastated. Best to delay the heartache.

His powerful body cut through the water in half the time hers had. He followed her trail through the reeds to the door hanging on its hinges. Stepping inside, his sharp gaze focused on her slumbering form, tangled, messy hair matted down her back, with the lower globes of each butt cheek visible. She was curled into the back of the couch trying to preserve as much heat as she could.

He padded quietly to her until he stood over her. The turmoil of his thoughts hit her like a raging storm. He sensed her agony and it flayed him, his guilt barely assuaged by his relief at finding her alive.

Flowing into the glorious nude male she adored ended her dream.

Maggie's eyes fluttered open at the sound of a muffled object hitting the floor. The floral pattern of the old couch greeted her. The flowers appeared grey and black in the dark cabin. With a start she twisted to look behind her with dread that it was all a cruel dream.

Stars exploded behind her eyes, stealing the view she'd have of Porter's thick thighs. Groaning she curled back into herself, her headache as mighty as when she'd went to sleep.

Porter dropped to his knees. "Maggie," hands stroked her hair, rubbed her chilled skin, "what's wrong?"

She didn't want the breakdown that took over, but she couldn't stop it. Tears poured down her cheeks.

"Maggie." Her name on his breath sounded as if he shared her torment.

He lifted her so he could slide underneath and cradle her. She snuggled in, absorbing his heat, still she cried.

He was real and he was really here, holding her.

"I was afraid," she murmured into his chest, "that my dream wasn't real and you weren't here."

"Oh god, Maggie. I'd never stop looking for you." He dropped kisses onto her head, stroking her back. His touch battled back a portion of the pain, but it was only temporary. "I'm so sorry."

"I know," she cried harder. "Me, too."

"Shh," he kissed her again. "You did absolutely nothing wrong; you have nothing to apologize for. I was the lunk." His soothing hands rubbed up and down her spine calming her distress. "Are you hurt?"

She nodded, the movement stabbing her brain. "Seamus shot me in the leg and head. I've healed around the bullets, but every movement rips new flesh."

The pungent smell of his anger overwhelmed the cabin. "He will die."

"I found a knife. With you here, we can cut them out."

His hands stalled. "Have you eaten?"

She answered verbally to spare her poor head. "I'm starving."

Hugging her tighter. "You won't heal properly without nutrition. The blood loss alone would incapacitate you and with Seamus out there…"

"He was caught in the blast," she said optimistically.

"It will only slow him down." He shifted her to the inside of the couch, handling her like a breakable doll. She felt like one. "I didn't take him seriously enough before and you paid for it. I won't do it again. But you need to eat."

Leaning over, he snatched up the bundle he'd had around his neck. The metallic odor hit her nose before it was completely unwrapped.

"I'm so glad to see that." Not nearly as elated as she was to wake up with Porter standing over her.

He slid out from under her, kneeling by the couch. His wrap of heat gone, goose bumps dotted her body. He handed her the grip of the gun. The

~238~

heft and weight was instantly familiar even if it was a model she'd never trained with.

Noting her ease around the weapon, he nodded. "I suspected I wouldn't have to tell you how to use one."

She smiled faintly, a shiver traveling down her down her body. Only this time it was due to the heated pride in his eyes.

He blinked, let out a deep exhale, his gaze sweeping her face. Dropping his head, he pressed his lips to hers, carrying it no further because of the agony emanating from her.

Sitting back on his heels, his face registered his unease leaving her. "I'm going to hunt. Call me for anything."

"I can't. The bullet's messing with my mind-speak."

He brushed a ratty lock of hair off her face. "I heard you when you were taken. You called for me."

Frowning, she remembered her desperate cry. "You were hundreds of miles away."

His full lips that she couldn't wait to explore again lifted in a smug smirk. "Our connection is just that strong." His grin faded as he considered the problem. "Howl if you need me."

She wanted to giggle, for the first time in two months; she settled for a wan smile. "If I need your help, you'll know it."

"Good enough." He stretched his shirt over her like a blanket. A metallic smell clung to it from his gun, but his essence among every fiber warmed her more than the material.

She watched him shift. Her fingers burrowed into his coarse fur. He licked her cheek as if to mark her before he left to hunt.

She wiggled into a more comfortable position, rearranging the shirt over her. The hand holding her gun rested on top of the shirt, pointed toward the door. Seamus probably wasn't stupid enough to use the front door, but it'd certainly be the easiest. And it took her mind off eating something with fur or feathers completely raw.

Chapter Seventeen

Porter crouched, his eyes gleaming silver under the moonlight. He detected trails of squirrels and rodents, but nothing definitive. His pride didn't want to present Maggie with a tiny mouse, but it was better than nothing. Her fatigue sapped his own energy; if he could take her physical torment, it'd be done.

Movement to the right captured his attention. He pounced, pinning a rabbit between his paws. A quick snap broke its neck. One bunny wouldn't be enough for Maggie; the bullets ripping into her flesh caused too much damage. Even without their connection, he'd have felt her pain, but he could see her suffering. The crystal blue eyes he dreamed about were glassy, the tremors in her body were not from the chill, and his normally vibrant, healthy mate weakened from the metal residing in her brain. Shifter's bodies couldn't push out foreign objects when they healed; she'd need constant nutrition to repair the damage that continued.

If he could make one more kill, he could bring them to her to eat and come back out to hunt for more. He left his catch by the base of a tree. Stalking through the growth, moving slowly, he spotted another rabbit several yards away.

A blast startled both him and his prey. The gunshot originated from the cabin. Porter's claws dug into the ground as he propelled toward the building.

A male's cry of rage erupted from the cabin.

He raced to the cabin, hearing snarls and another gunshot, followed by the clatter of metal hitting the wooden floor.

Porter tore through the door to find a burly wolf entangled within a set of pale limbs. Maggie's arms wrapped around the neck of the wolf. The creature writhed, his hind claws scraping for a foothold, but Maggie's brief training was enough to catch Seamus off guard. He hadn't been prepared to fight a female who knew how to fight back.

Blood dripped from Maggie's legs; she'd been clawed severely. Porter leapt the distance, but Seamus had sensed him.

Risking the shift, Seamus flowed into his other form, the shift loosening Maggie's hold. He wrestled away from her, kicking out at Porter.

Porter snapped at the foot, but missed. Seamus continued kicking, Maggie's arms snaked around his neck, but he exploded backward. The combination of her lunge and his movement sent her reeling. She quickly recovered.

Seamus bared his teeth and dived for the gun. Maggie did the same. The crack of their skulls resonated through the room, sickening Porter.

Maggie dropped, her limbs twitching. Disorientated, Seamus shook his head, feeling along the floor for the gun. Before he could find it, Porter jumped on him, latching onto his neck, the crunch of trachea under his teeth satisfying.

Seamus punched his flanks, Porter bit harder, blood gushing into his mouth. *Nothing* would release his hold. Seamus tried rolling, Porter sawed his jaws. The male gripped Porter's head, his weakened grip unable to budge him. The other wolf's eyes lolled back into his head and he sagged with defeat. With no air and a bout of sudden anemia, the maniac was left with no fight.

Finally, Seamus fell limp. Porter hung on to ensure the bastard was out. When he was confident, he released and rushed to Maggie's side.

Maggie's legs and arm flopped, her eyes rolled back. She wasn't recovering.

Spinning around, he frantically scanned the room. His first priority was Maggie, she needed help. But it'd do no good if they left Seamus here to come after her another day.

Spotting the knife on the counter, he ran to it, shifting as he moved. The medium-sized blade, while slightly better than a steak knife, would require more time, but it'd do.

Seamus' thick neck did not sever easily, the guy had to wear a size twenty collar. He sawed through tissue, but he had to get creative with the bone. A combination of hacking, tugging, ripping and he separated Seamus' ugly mug from his thick body.

There was no time to relish his success, only Maggie mattered. The bullet in her head prevented healing, Porter worried that it'd tax her healing abilities past the point of no return.

He located his shirt and wrapped his gun back in it, and tied it onto Maggie. As gently as he could, he hefted her into his arms so her head rested on his shoulder instead of dangling down to bounce as he ran, increasing internal damage.

Porter carefully stepped through the doorway and took off at a run.

***

His lungs burned, screaming for him to stop and rest, but Porter kept going. After several miles, Maggie had gone still. Was she recovering, or was her brain giving up on life? She was desperately depleted of nutrition and he couldn't afford to stop and nourish himself. He'd circled the lake until he found the trail he'd taken from his pickup and made a beeline back to his truck.

Porter pumped his legs, dodging trees and branches. His focus remained on the path in front of him—tripping was not an option.

Shortly after dawn, his pickup came into view. Porter slowed to evaluate the safety of running naked out of the trees, carrying an unconscious, mostly nude female, both of them covered in dried blood.

A few other cars were parked in the area. One couple stood beside their Jeep, checking each other's packs. Porter's sides heaved, but he remained as silent as possible while he was puffing like a cigar smoker.

Maggie's limbs hung. Porter hugged her closer, his gaze focused on the couple.

Fucking leave!

Maggie groaned. Porter's breath froze. Shit.

The man looked back over his shoulder, the woman asked him what was wrong. Porter prayed he was deep enough in the trees that they weren't visible—and that Maggie wouldn't utter another sound.

The dude shrugged and the couple headed toward a trailhead to begin their hike. Porter took a step forward and froze again when a car pulled in.

What. The? Was the ass crack of dawn the best time to hike?

The car had one occupant and sat idling.

Porter's muscles tensed until tremors traveled through his body. His phone was in his pickup; he was worthless until the coast was clear.

The drone of another engine sounded in the distance. A second car rolled in, aiming for the idling car. The driver pulled alongside, Porter heard voices, saw the exchange of a package and an envelope. The drivers continued to discuss business in hushed tones.

Sweet Mother! Finish the fucking drug deal and get the hell outta here!

Deal done, the drivers pulled away and left.

Hearing no new engines, he trotted to his pickup. Holding Maggie gingerly, he squatted to dig for his keys and hit unlock. He couldn't stand the thought of not holding her, wondering if she'd grow cold and if she'd warm to life again.

It took some fancy maneuvering, but she lay across the passenger seat, her head on his bare leg. He fired up his truck, threw on his t-shirt and spun out of the parking lot.

He set the cruise control again. Half-naked, filthy, and covered in dried blood, it'd be game over if he was pulled over. He drove, twisted in knots about Maggie and giving himself a spit bath with his shirt.

He grabbed his phone and hit the last number he'd called.

It rang to voicemail and Porter repeated the same procedure as the day before. Maggie shuttered next to him. Her breathing rate sped up until she panted, then slowed, ending on a groan. He stroked her shoulder. It seemed to help.

"Fucking-A, Denlan!" Jace raged on the other end. "We can't find Maggie with you dialing in."

"I have her. She's hurt." Porter rattled off all the details he knew to the suddenly attentive

Guardian on the other end. "I need to get her to you without driving through a populated area."

"I think I know how Seamus got to that gas station where she blew the van. There's no roads around it, only through, but if you can get by the gas station without attracting attention, stay on the same highway. You can take the furthest south bridge across the river. It's the less populated area of Freemont. We'll notify Doc and meet you at the main road so you can follow us into headquarters."

"Seamus—"

"We'll get a couple of guys out there for cleanup." Jace paused for a heartbeat. "I wish you woulda saved him for me."

"Not a chance. My only regret is that he didn't suffer more."

"He's done. We'll help you ferret out any shifter who helped him. I'll accept them as my consolation prize."

"I think you'll have to wait in line for Mage," Porter drawled.

"Right. Good work, Denlan." Jace disconnected.

A compliment? From Jace? Admittedly, Porter was relieved. Maggie didn't need shit from the two of them, and Porter planned on hanging around for more than a while; he would be the mouse on her sticky trap.

He steered through the curves of the country roads. The silence crushed in around him until he thought he'd crawl out of his skin and climb the walls.

Maggie's chest started heaving, her eyelids fluttered like she struggled to consciousness, then she sagged against him again. He set the cruise another five miles an hour faster. What happened when she could no longer heal herself?

He started talking. Her trembling subsided to faint quivers under his hand. Recounting the days they'd spent apart, he told her about all the decisions he'd had to make, the people who supported him. The assholes who didn't. How he planned to deal with them.

Next came the litanies of "I'm sorry" and "I miss you", but her agitation grew. Switching to song with his scratchy voice, he serenaded her with any and every country song he remembered. All those hours of throwing walls together and listening to the radio paid off. Maggie calmed again and he made the long drive.

Aw hell. He was running low on gas, was barely gonna make it. Unrolling his gun from his plaid, he spread the shirt over her. It was broad daylight as he drove through Freemont. Singing under his breath to maintain a lower profile and still soothe her, he did his best to park off kilter at stop lights to prevent casual glances that would spot h.

At last, he crossed the river, his gas gauge bottoming out. They passed Pale Moonlight and the view of rundown West Creek had never been so beautiful.

Porter was on his twentieth Garth Brooks song, fretting about running on fumes, when he spotted a black Denali parked off the side of the road, running. The taillights flashed on and the vehicle pulled out. Porter remained behind them. Once they turned off the highway, the SUV kicked into high gear and he clung to their bumper all the way.

Chapter Eighteen

The gurney Maggie lay on rolled as fast as its little wheels allowed, being pushed by three shifters and whatever the slight young woman was. She smelled like a bit of each species. As long as she was vetted by the Guardians and she had the potential to help Maggie, Porter didn't care.

A tall, lanky male Jace called Doc had emerged from the lodge as soon as their wheels puffed clouds of dirt skidding to a stop. Armana was hot on his heels. He'd taken charge, directing Porter without pretense. Jace fell in line to push the cot and the woman began strapping wires to Maggie.

Seeing medical devices strapped to a shifter, Maggie most of all, disturbed Porter. His people were embracing technology, modern medicine included. That Maggie's life hung in dire enough circumstances to require the use of it...

They strode through the halls of the Guardians' training center. He recalled his time in the interrogation room, the cell where he and Maggie had spent the night. His mate lived here.

Trained here. She might very well land herself in these kind of circumstances again with her job as a Guardian.

It was more than a job. It was her life. It was her.

And he loved her.

They piled into a sterile, white room—an infirmary of sorts. Supplies had already been set up along the counters. Doc went straight for them.

"Mr. Denlan," the older shifter said as he rummaged through the items, "pull up a chair next to the cot."

Porter searched for a chair, found one against the wall, and did exactly as Doc instructed.

The male acted in a way that suggested he'd spent much time among frantic loved ones and knew how to communicate with them.

"I'm going to sedate her. Not only will it be more comfortable, but her mind won't work against us by trying to rouse her." Doc inserted a long needle into Maggie's upper arm.

Armana arranged a sheet over her. A red, heated patch of skin on Maggie's thigh caught his attention. "She was shot in the thigh, too. Said the bullet was still in her."

Jace swore; Doc acknowledged the news, his main concern Maggie's brain.

"Ana," Doc spoke, as he arranged power tools that Porter was probably more familiar with, "set up the blood exchange. Clamp it off after a minute. I only want to nourish her enough to tolerate surgery. Once I'm complete and we need to heal her, we'll transfer more. Only from Mr. Stockwell."

"A transfusion?" Armana asked.

Doc's eyes crinkled slightly. "Exactly. Performed the shifter way. We don't need to worry about transfusion reactions."

Porter could give her first blood; his mating instincts were satisfied with that. Logically, he knew he needed a few steak meals before he could supply her with as much as she needed. As long as the other donor was her brother, he talked his mating ego down. Grim lines etched into Jace's features. The male's concern over his sister rolled off him in waves. The guy needed to feel like he was doing something, too.

Ana softly talked him through the procedure. She didn't need to. A crowbar could pierce his skin and he wouldn't flinch as long as it helped Maggie.

The healer's hands moved over her head, his fingertips lightly probing her scalp.

"Why didn't the bullets go through?" Jace broke into Doc's concentration.

The older male ignored him until he was satisfied with what he felt around Maggie's head. "The leg shot was probably from farther away, and the head shot…" Doc shook his head. "Bad luck and our hard shifter heads."

"The tubing's clamped off," Ana announced. She disconnected Porter and beckoned Jace over.

Grudgingly, Porter gave up his seat. Standing up, a wave of light headedness passed through him. Add some bacon to those steak meals. Maybe a few medium rare burgers. But he wouldn't eat until Maggie was at the table with him.

Without taking his hands off her, he moved around the table to the other side. Clasping her limp hand, he stayed on his feet.

Doc pulled down protective glasses. "This won't be pleasant. If either of you interfere, you'll be removed and it'll delay her procedure."

Jace and Porter nodded in confirmation; Armana studied them both intently. He was Maggie's mate, Jace was her brother, but Doc's role as her healer trumped both of them and Armana would make sure of it.

"Hold her hair out of the way," Doc said to Ana. "Shaving it will just make a mess."

A small bone saw whirred to life.

Porter squeezed Maggie's hand, stroked her forearm. The sounds emanating from Doc's work sickened his stomach. There was sawing wood and there was sawing bone, and Porter never wanted to hear the latter again.

He focused on Maggie's fingers, each second felt like two hours had passed. Jace sat across from him staring at the floor. Armana stood at the foot of the bed, her eyes narrowed on Doc, as if she wanted to know the millisecond something went wrong.

Maggie hadn't eaten in a couple of days, had sustained major injuries, but she had his blood flowing through her veins. They weren't vampires, but it had to be enough for her to heal.

A slight metal clang jerked Porter's head up. The bullet was out.

"Ana, hook Mr. Stockwell up, please." Doc wrapped gauze around Maggie's head; he caught Porter's eye. "I put the section I cut back into place—less bone for her body to generate." He took a deep breath, visibly relaxed, and wiped his hands off. "Now, let's take a look at her leg."

***

Maggie drifted light as a feather rising out of a deep sleep. Sweet Mother, she was uncomfortable. Groaning, she rolled over. She made it as far as her side, weak as a newborn puppy.

This would do. Except her hair tickled. Reaching up, she batted at the offender. Her hand swiped soft material that was wrapped around her head.

What the…?

Opening her eyes, her first sight was a haggard Porter sleeping in an office chair, slumped against the wall. A long piece of gauze dangled from her fingers.

Getting shot. Seamus!

She flung up, and flopped back down. Porter appeared at her side. She sensed her mother and Jace, but her attention was sluggish moving away from her mate.

"Hey." She offered a tired smile, it was the best she could do in her weakened state.

Stress visibly drained out of his expression. "Hey yourself."

"Is he dead?"

Porter's gaze soaked her in. "He lost his head."

"Good." Her own body relaxed. "Good." Only then did she cast a glance around. Her mom, worry still tainting her eyes, held a tray full of meat that made Maggie's fangs drool. Jace hung a foot behind Porter, like he felt Armana and Porter took priority.

Before she could say anything to them, her mother barked orders. "Porter, prop her bed up. There's a lever somewhere. Jace bring the side table over. She needs food."

"It smells delicious." The head of the cot rose while the crisp, white sheet slid down. She tucked the ends behind her. Nothing was going to stand in the way of her and the red meat on the tray.

Popping bacon into her mouth, she hardly chewed before swallowing. Nitrates were a shifter's best friend. "Fill me in. I remember Seamus sneaking into the cabin and I plugged a round into his ratty hide."

She speared a piece of steak someone had the foresight to cut up for her, otherwise she'd be face first in her dish. She was *starving*.

"When I ran back," Porter explained, "you had Seamus in a choke hold. He shifted to get out of it and dived for the gun. You met him headfirst."

"That explains the black out. I don't remember any of that." They had superhero hearing if they could make out her words around the food.

"You weren't recovering, I raced back here, and Doc dug the lead out of you…"

She stopped chewing, sensing Porter withheld an important detail.

"Three days ago," he finished.

"Three days?"

"Porter's not left your side." Her mom pushed the plate closer to prompt her to keep eating.

"Your mom hardly did, either," Porter countered.

"You guys are making me sound like a slacker," Jace grumbled. He tapped Maggie's foot. "Good to see you up. I gotta get back out in the field."

Maggie gave him a little wave before he left, and looked between her mom and Porter. "Why so long? I'm a shifter."

Armana chuckled. "We're not immortal, dear. Just hard to kill. If you had been able to get back here immediately and had the bullets dug out, you'd have healed in a day. But…" Her voice caught, her eyes were haunted.

"But I'm here, Ma. I'm okay. Just really hungry."

Armana wiped away glistening tears. "I lost Bane and Keve. I almost cost myself Jace, and then you—" She cut herself off, blew out a gusty breath. With a wry chuckle, she shook her head. "Now you're both Guardians and I'll worry for the rest of my life."

Maggie dropped her fork and grabbed her mom's hand. "I know. I wish I could squirrel your worry away." Her glance flicked to Porter. "But it's who I am."

He brushed her hair back. Ick, it must be a greasy mess. "I know who you are, Mage." His ragged whisper betrayed his emotion.

Her mom patted her hand and pulled away. "I'll leave you two to talk."

Maggie expected a hard look thrown Porter's way, not the loving motherly expression with a grateful nod from Porter.

Maggie quirked a brow watching her mom walk out. "You two must've had plenty of time to talk in three days."

"She knows how I feel about you." Scratching the scruff that should be called a full-fledged beard, he propped a hip on the cot. "I'm so sorry for dragging you into this. For Seam—"

She stopped him with a finger pressed over his lips, the dichotomy of his coarse, yet soft facial hair tickling her skin. "We've already covered this. Let's not keep circling back."

Heat flared in his eyes; he bared his teeth and snapped at her digit.

Pulling her hand back with a gasp, she almost regretted it, wanted to know how it'd feel if he caught her.

His hand snaked around her wrist. She would've been dragged to his chest, but the food tray rattled and he eased up to cradle her hand in his. "I'm afraid, Mage," his thumb swirled in her palm, "you're stuck with me."

Oh, the naughty ideas that came to mind when their skin touched, when he teased with sensations that could be imagined elsewhere.

The meaning of his statement sunk in. "What about Lobo Springs?"

A heavy shoulder lifted in a casual shrug; she knew it was anything but. "It'll be fine without me. There's some good shifters who'll pick up the slack."

Good shifters who wanted him as the mayor, who trusted him to see them through the turmoil Seamus left behind.

"What about the moles who helped Seamus sneak around and find out about you and me?"

"I'll help the Guardians sniff them out. I can do that from here."

Maggie stared at her plate. Porter. Here.

His thumb ceased movement, his grip loosened. "Do you want me here?"

"Yes, of course. It's just…we're going from meeting each other, to broken up, to living together.

I feel like I should put a stop to it, slow us down." Porter's jaw clenched, his brow furrowed. "But the truth is, I missed you so much, I never want you to leave. Is that desperate?"

A slow, sexy grin spread across his face. "I'm desperate times ten. I've filled up Sanders shop for the next year making furniture."

Her grin matched his…until it faded. "You can't just desert Lobo Springs."

He blinked, thinking about it. Proof leaving the community bothered him. "I can help them find someone to take over from here. You come first. Always."

A voice spoke from the hallway. "There might be another way."

Commander Fitzsimmons strode in, Bennett on his heels. Both males stopped short. Porter kept his hold on her, an inquiring expression on his rugged face.

Bennett crossed his arms, his blue eyes serious. "It'd require some commuting, until you're fully trained."

The commander, always straightforward, thankfully got to the point. Maggie was bursting with curiosity. "I discussed with the Synod the problem with coverage we're facing. Villages hours away like yours," he tilted his head toward Porter, "are having problems that need immediate attention. A village with as many clans and packs as Lobo Springs would benefit from having a Guardian within town limits."

"I'd be stationed there?" She'd move to the home of her birth, away from the friends she'd made in the last couple of months, and her family? But she'd be with Porter.

"She'd have to leave her family and friends," Porter said as if reading her mind. "I can't do that to her."

The heavy weight of Bennett's and the commander's stare rested on her. They waited on her acquiescence. Either one had the right to order her to follow their directives, but they lay the decision at her feet. Not Porter's, not her mother's, but hers.

"I'm a big girl now. With today's technology, Ma's just a Facetime call away and I'm sure I get vacation days." The commander nodded. "I think we can make this work. Porter?"

He seemed surprised at her quick agreement. "Yeah, of course. You'd really move in with me?"

"This...is an amazing opportunity." She faced her boss. "You'd do that for me?"

Commander Fitzsimmons' face didn't twitch because, duh, he didn't get made to do anything he didn't want to. "You wouldn't be there alone. By the time your training's complete, we'll have found another Guardian to be your partner."

Bennett ran his hands through his hair, a move he did when he was in deep thought. Or out of frustration. Or all the time. "And we're plotting our area to determine stations to start placing

Guardians. We can't all live out here and provide service over hundreds of miles."

Maggie reined in her excitement. "About what happened...how I failed my training..." Failed all of you.

The commander's features didn't change, Bennett's expression turned perplexed. Sweet Mother, how was she ever supposed to be as bad ass as them?

"You went for a run," Bennett began. "And yeah, maybe it wasn't the best idea to leave the wards when the feral asshole still hadn't been found. But you passed a message to us, then got away from Seamus while severely wounded. No humans detected our presence—despite blowing a gas station into the next county. You're alive, Seamus ended up dead. I don't call that a failure."

"There's a few teaching moments we can extract from the experience." The commander's eyes twinkled (once) in amusement.

"We work predominantly in pairs for a reason," Bennett added. "All of us have faced death and only got out of the situation with help. Don't beat yourself up about it. Learn and move on."

They were comparing her to them. Awe—some. Her two months of training while pining for a male had made her feel less than. Less than Guardian worthy. Less than born for the job. Less than prepared to defend herself.

So when shifters like Bennett and the commander not quite praised her for a situation she would've never imagined two and a half months ago? She'd take it.

Porter cleared his throat, bemusement leaving his expression. "Won't it be a conflict of interest if one of the Guardians happens to be the mayor's mate?"

Maggie's high hopes plummeted. Porter's position was secure as far as she knew, but how would it go over when he announced that Guardians would be stationed in town, and oh by the way, one's my mate. Suspicion could destroy what he'd worked so hard for.

Bennett acknowledged Porter's concern with respect. "Anyone who has a problem with it can suck it."

Commander Fitzsimmons inclined his head in agreement. "They voted you in because they trusted you. You obviously care about what they think. Take a vote, tell 'em you'll step down, whatever. If they don't feel like you're abusing your relationship, it won't be an issue."

"What you're saying is," Porter said, "the Guardians take no stance in the matter, as long as peace is preserved, and it doesn't create more work for you?"

Bennett grinned. "Nailed it. See you got this politician thing down."

"Nah. I'm just a woodworker who's not insane. Right now, that's all the position requires."

"It's settled then." Commander Fitzsimmons jutted his square jaw toward Porter. "Denlan, before you head back to Lobo Springs, we have a couple of projects for you. Maggie, when you feel up to it, Doc said you can head back to your quarters whenever you're ready. Tomorrow it's back to training."

Yessss. Maggie forced herself not to jump out of bed and run to her room. After the two Guardians left, she batted her lashes coyly at Porter. "I need a shower desperately. Want to join me?"

A slow, sexy grin spread across his face. Fire blazed in his dark eyes. "Show me the way, Mage."

Epilogue

Porter finished tapping the last piece of trim in and stood. The room turned out better than he'd thought. Who was he kidding? He knew he'd transform his bachelor pad into an aesthetic living area his mate would enjoy. Ten months he'd had to transform his house into a home while Maggie finished training.

His garage had been expanded for his shop and contained all of his equipment. The nights Maggie was called away for work, he'd wander out there to tinker around. The living area now sported a TV with something called a Roku for streaming shows and movies built in. The beast filled half the wall. Real furniture faced the TV, ready for them to turn into zombies when Maggie's favorite shows were on.

Armana had been his shopping buddy for furnishings. She knew Maggie's tastes in home décor and delighted in mothering the hell out of him. His mom had been gone so long, he'd forgotten how comforting it was to have a maternal figure around. With Maggie steeped in learning and Jace with his own mate, Armana adopted Porter in seconds when he'd asked if could get her opinion on style and color. She hadn't gone as far as moving back, even though Porter offered to build her a guest house on his land. Too many memories, too soon, she'd said.

Too far away from Jace and Maggie, he'd suspected. He had gone ahead and drawn up plans for a small structure because once Maggie resided here full time, Armana didn't need to camp on the new couch.

Tossing his tools away, he figured he'd have time to clean up and throw on his "dress" clothes—jeans without stains and a solid colored button-up. Everyone would be showing up within the hour for the official mating ceremony.

Including his mate.

They'd maintained a long-distance relationship, spending any free time together in each other's arms. His place, or her room, didn't matter. But he hadn't pushed for the ceremony. It wasn't totally an altruistic move. She had her Guardian commitment, and he wanted her to have time to learn all about herself and how shifters lived.

Then there was the mating frenzy. Hours upon hours of straight up sex. Then rest. Then more sex. It was a time to meld with each other, become a complete couple. Their bites staked the claim on the other's soul, the ceremony completed the bond. That was the only area he was being selfish. Porter didn't want any constraints on their mating time together.

Being happily mated males, her superiors understood and granted Maggie two weeks to move and settle in before she eased into work. Her partner, a vampire they hadn't met yet, would situate himself up here afterward. The brainchild of Commander Fitzsimmons and the Synod meant to integrate vampires and shifters, even in the most rural places.

Then Maggie would begin her service as the Lobo Springs area Guardian and Porter would begin calming the shifters in town about the vampire who'd be living and working among them.

As long as the guy watched Maggie's back and didn't mess with his town's people, Porter's give-a-shit meter hit bottom.

He raced through the shower and by the time he threw on his clothes, a car was pulling into the garage. She was at the door ripping it open before he reached it.

Hell, she was sexy. He'd never tire of seeing her in those cargo pants that accentuated her hips and tight tech shirt that molded over her breasts. And when she wore all her weapons...he was lost to lust.

Catching her in his arms, their mouths pressed together. It'd been two whole weeks since they'd been together, but it felt longer. Thank the Sweet Mother for the internet and phone sex.

Maggie broke the kiss and pulled his shirt over his head.

"Whoa." He didn't want to whoa, he wanted Maggie to finish what she was doing. "We have a ceremony to get to."

She leaned in to nibble his neck and unbuttoned his jeans. Helpless to give into her, he worked on her clothing.

"I told them it didn't start for a couple more hours."

A slow grin spread across his face. "You needed to get something outta the way?"

No answer, only kissing her way farther down, taking his pants with.

"I like your planning."

Stopping to grin up at him, she blinked then looked around. "Look at this place." Standing up, she wandered around their house, eyes wide. "It's gorgeous and OMG, is that a sixty-inch TV?"

"Ask and ye shall receive." He finished stepping out of his pants, his erection straining to get to her.

Turning when she heard the movement, she grinned, biting her lip when she spied his arousal. "You did all this for me?"

"You're everything to me. I love you and want you to be happy here."

Warmth infused her features. "I love you, too. You'll have to give me a tour—later."

"After we christen the new couch." He growled, lunging for her and swinging her up into his arms.

Her laughter turned to gasps as he went to work showing her just how much she meant to him.

Thank you for reading. I'd love to know what you thought. Please consider leaving a review at the retailor the book was purchased from.
Marie

Ancient Ties
Book 2, Pale Moonlight
To be released January 2017

*Kaitlyn Savoy loves her job as a Guardian,
the police force for vampires, shifters, and hybrids.
As a shifter, work would be so much easier if she
could shift to her wolf form and not pass out
afterward.*

*Fellow Guardian Chayton Delorme is
dismayed that a defunct shifter is his mate, and
Kaitlyn doesn't even seem to know it. He swore an
oath to his family to keep his bloodline strong, and
while he can't deny Kaitlyn's good at her job, she's
not mate material for him.*

*When he's trapped and tortured by feral
shifters, she's his only chance. Kaitlyn must dig
down to the trauma of her past because she'll need
all her abilities to save his body and soul.*

Rourke
New Vampire Disorder, book two
To be released September 2016

She watches him from the shadows. He embodies her nightmare in a dark, seductive package.

Grace Otto was saved as a baby by a human family when her vampire parents were slaughtered. She was raised with love away from the monsters who hide in the night. When her human family is murdered, her nightmare male is there, walking among their remains. She should run from him, but she desires justice.

Rourke senses he's being watched. Only when he catches the lovely female whose scent calls to him, he discovers their pasts are linked in a horrific way. To find out what happened to Grace's loved ones, he'll need to hunt down the demons of their past.

About the Author

Marie Johnston lives in the upper-Midwest with her husband, four kids, and an old cat. Deciding to trade in her lab coat for a laptop, she's writing down all the tales she's been making up in her head for years. An avid reader of paranormal romance, these are the stories hanging out and waiting to be told between the demands of work, home, and the endless chauffeuring that comes with children.

Sign-up for my newsletter at:
www.mariejohnstonwriter.com

Follow Marie Johnston Writer on Facebook and @mjohnstonwriter on Twitter.

Also by Marie Johnston

The Sigma Menace:
Fever Claim (Book 1)
Primal Claim (Book 2)
True Claim (Book 3)
Reclaim (Book 3.5)
Lawful Claim (Book 4)
Pure Claim (Book 5)

New Vampire Disorder:
Demetrius (Book 1)
Rourke (Book 2) released September 20116

63440070R00150

Made in the USA
Charleston, SC
04 November 2016